Pulphuse
FICTION MAGAZINE

Issue Thirty

Magazine Editor
Dean Wesley Smith

A WMG Publishing Magazine

wmg
PUBLISHING

MORE FROM PULPHOUSE

Jingle My Bells

No Way: Totally Twisted Tales

Run!! Creatures, Critters, and Pulphousers...

Snot-Nosed Aliens

That's Really Messed Up

There'll Be Blue Popcorn Without You!

Three Sheets to the Wind

Twisted Robots, Oh, My!

STORIES FROM THE ORIGINAL PULPHOUSE

Stories from the Original Pulphouse: A Fiction Magazine

Stories from Pulphouse: The Hardback Magazine

ALSO BY
DEAN WESLEY SMITH

COLD POKER GANG

Kill Game

Cold Call

Calling Dead

Bad Beat

Dead Hand

Freezeout

Ace High

Burn Card

Heads Up

Ring Game

Bottom Pair

Case Card

THE POKER BOY UNIVERSE

POKER BOY

The Slots of Saturn: A Poker Boy Novel

They're Back: A Poker Boy Short Novel

Luck Be Ladies: A Poker Boy Collection

Playing a Hunch: A Poker Boy Collection

A Poker Boy Christmas: A Poker Boy Collection

GHOST OF A CHANCE

The Poker Chip: A Ghost of a Chance Novel

The Christmas Gift: A Ghost of a Chance Novel

The Free Meal: A Ghost of a Chance Novel

The Cop Car: A Ghost of a Chance Novella

The Deep Sunset: A Ghost of a Chance Novel

MARBLE GRANT

The First Year: A Marble Grant Novel

Time for Cool Madness: Six Crazy Marble Grant Stories

PAKHET JONES

The Big Tom: A Packet Jones Short Novel

Big Eyes: A Packet Jones Short Novel

THUNDER MOUNTAIN

Thunder Mountain

Monumental Summit

Avalanche Creek

The Edwards Mansion

Lake Roosevelt

Warm Springs

Melody Ridge

Grapevine Springs

The Idanha Hotel

The Taft Ranch

Tombstone Canyon

Dry Creek Crossing

Hot Springs Meadow

Green Valley

SEEDERS UNIVERSE

Dust and Kisses: A Seeders Universe Prequel Novel

Against Time

Sector Justice

Morning Song

The High Edge

Star Mist

Star Rain

Star Fall

Starburst

Rescue Two

Pulphouse Fiction Magazine Issue #30
Published by WMG Publishing Inc.
Cover and interior design copyright © 2024 WMG Publishing Inc.
Cover art copyright © Ellerslie | Depositphotos
Small creature we call Thumper copyright © beutoszig |Depositphotos

TABLE OF CONTENTS

SHORT STORIES

Pulphouse Fiction Magazine
A WMG Publishing Magazine

Editor	Executive Editor	Director of Operations
Dean Wesley Smith	Kristine Kathryn Rusch	Stephanie Writt

FROM THE EDITOR'S DESK
ANOTHER ROUND NUMBER

When we relaunched *Pulphouse Fiction Magazine* thirty issues ago, if we could have seen the bumps and problems that were ahead, I doubt we would have done it.

We started off quarterly and were doing just great right up to the pandemic when we paused publication. Actually we paused a bunch of stuff at WMG Publishing to make sure the company and employees made it through.

When this magazine restarted, we had decided to go to six issues a year instead of four. And that worked great right up to the day in October of 2022 that I woke up blind. So we paused the magazine again, took a hard look at what we wanted to do, and then restarted it as a monthly in the fall of 2023 after I had recovered most of my sight.

We changed format and also purposely made the issues simple in layout to make sure we could get the monthly schedule on track.

We had three issues in the pipeline when I fell running a 5k charity run and smashed my shoulder, ended up in surgery, and could not type for three months. We managed to keep the magazine on schedule during that time and we were coming back when we had a business crisis in WMG Publishing and had to make a lot of changes.

But we are still monthly and on schedule.

And we hope with either issue thirty-one or thirty-two, the look and feel of the magazine will be more fun, as Pulphouse is supposed to be.

As it used to be back with the first issue.

To say it has been a bumpy road to get to this issue is a laughable understatement. But here we are and looking into a bright future.

Thank you all for being a part of this crazy journey so far. I hope you stay with us for whatever comes next.

DEAN WESLEY SMITH
LAS VEGAS, NEVADA

LIVE THE PULPHOUSE LIFE!

Grab your Pulphouse mug and fill it with your favorite beverage and lounge in your coziest chair with the Thumper pillow while you read the latest issue of *Pulphouse*.

Want to mark off the date when your next issue will arrive? Get the *Pulphouse* calendar featuring some of our favorite *Pulphouse* cartoons!

Find all this and so much more at the *Pulphouse Fiction Magazine* online store at:

http://pulphousemagazine.com

The Pillow
(22" X 22")

The Mug
(15 OZ.)

And say hi to Thump while you're there.

Pulphouse

FICTION MAGAZINE

Issue Thirty

JOE CRON

Joe Cron writes some fantastic science fiction full of very human characters in very strange settings. And I wanted this story to lead off this issue because as science fiction goes, it is flat out weird and this perfect for these pages.

Joe has spent forty years in writing, acting, and music. He has performed on the piano in all types of bands, combos, and orchestras, and on stage in over fifty theatrical productions.

Other activities in Joe's past include a stint as a radio disc jockey and writing a wide variety of projects for venues ranging from theatre to corporate newsletter columns. You can find out a ton more about his books and writing at joecron.com.

THE FINAL FALL

JOE CRON

B arney Escondido sat in an old, creaky rocking chair on
the covered front porch of his friend, Nate Dallinger.
The two were buddies since forever, and neither had other
family to speak of, so this was an established scene. Nate
rocked gently in a similar chair a few feet away from Barney,
the two angled a touch toward each other, but with the front
door between. Barney was in the chair on the right, so to his
left was the space in front of the door and then Nate, and to
his right was a small outdoor end table with a tumbler of rum
and root beer. Barney savored a sip and set it back down.

Both men had small devices on their left ear. Barney's
head-up display splashed the message VISITORS
APPROACHING, with a number that showed one, two, then
quickly zipped up to seven.

"Ah," said Barney.

"Got it," said Nate. With minimal effort, he reached down
into a cloth pouch draped over the arm of his chair and

I

produced a remote control, black, oblong, and slightly larger than his hand.

"Still not using vocal?" said Barney.

"For some things, I prefer pressing metal to metal," said Nate.

The house was mid-twentieth-century Earth, like many in that neighborhood. There were large areas of the biggest cities that catered to specific historic architectures, and that was a reasonably popular one. Nate's house had thick, grey, shingle siding that Barney admitted had character, though Barney's own tastes were somewhere around eight hundred years later.

The current year was another millennium past all that, and Barney, Nate, and a billion others were on a planet ship called Galactos Mauve. It was one of a massive fleet of Galactos ships, in the color series. Hundreds of mechanical planets, all named with a color. Theirs was Galactos Mauve. There were so many that people got sick of saying "Galactos" for all of them and shortened it to "G," such that Barney and Nate were on G Mauve.

While somewhat smaller, everything else about these ships was built to mimic a real planet, and their systems were not completely self-sustaining, but close. G Mauve was approaching its first maintenance cycle, at a thousand years.

Trouble was, they had no way to perform it. That maintenance required a piece of equipment that was not to be found anywhere on G Mauve. Not functioning, that is. At one time, there were quite a few around the globe. Dozens, at least. But no more. And no way to get more.

That was all because of the singularity that swept their

galaxy hundreds of years earlier. There was an enormous array of Galactos ships forming an immense system, and they interacted constantly, as some of the ships became specialized. Horban fruit, for instance, was incredibly expensive to produce because of environmental peculiarities, but hugely popular, so rather than establish a proper growing environment on every planet ship, a few would become dedicated to specific things like that. G Mauve was not a specialist ship, and that helped it survive this long, but the singularity doomed everyone's fate when it collided with G Mauve.

It did a number of things, but the two with the most pressing influence on Barney's situation that day—and everyone on G Mauve—were that it flung them many galaxies away from the Galactos array they were in, or any others; and that it catastrophically damaged a vanishingly rare material known as wexium, and that was in chips that ran equipment that performed the millennium maintenance.

Barney took another sip of his delectable rum and root beer, and inhaled the cool, fresh air. Following Earth's calendar—and the Galactos ships typically replicated Earth in most ways, unless, again, there was a specialized reason not to—it was December 22, 3767. G Mauve had seasons, but mild winters, so it was slightly cool on the last day of autumn, but still shirtsleeve weather. Barney and Nate were both in their regular, comfortable jeans and long-sleeve shirts, looking out from the porch over Nate's front lawn and the road that curved along past it. Nate's house was in a curious position, geographically. To the left was an enormous, nearly vertical rock face from an abrupt plateau, and the road curved out from around that and past Nate's house in less than a thousand feet. On the far side of the road, a river.

The house was at the edge of Ganlisburg, the primary metropolis on G Mauve, and the road came down from the suburbs on the plateau, so between the edge of the plateau and the river, it was a primary traffic funnel on that side of town. Nothing of note, normally, but just recently, it created a sort of phenomenon. Just recently, they all learned they're about to die.

At 6:04 p.m., and thirty-six seconds, to be exact. It was a little past eleven, so some hours to go. Nothing would necessarily die at that exact moment, but the planet would. All technical systems of any kind were about to shut down. No power to anything. Instant, complete darkness and silence, followed quickly by the cold of deep space.

It was part of life on that ship that everyone knew it couldn't last forever, and not even until some traveling species discovered them adrift. They had minimal power and maneuverability, but that was only made for positioning within the Galactos array. Useless for interstellar travel, even within a galaxy, and they were in the vast space between galaxies, were no technology they even knew of could reach. At the same time, they'd been that way for more than three hundred years, and no generation really expected to be the last. Certainly not without more warning than they had.

A person came in view from behind the rock face, walking briskly. There were cars in the road, parked and abandoned over the past couple days. Not solid, but hindering the roadway. No moving traffic. The person was in the road, but on Barney's side of the cars.

"Sighted," said Nate.

"Right," said Barney.

Within moments, a second and third person came into view. Eventually, seven, just as the head-up display had indicated. Barney straightened up in his chair.

"Don't get nervous," said Nate. He thumbed a button on the remote he was holding.

"If you say so," said Barney.

It was plain to see that all seven were armed. A wide variety of items from firearms to clubs. There were five men and two women. Turning the corner and discovering they were at the edge of town seemed to invigorate the lot. A couple of them jumped and skipped around a little, and all were vocalizing various whoops and hollers as they moved down the road.

Barney's head-up display flashed VISITORS AT 500 FT.

On cue, Nate said, "Got it. But they're visual now." He put his thumb on another button and pressed.

Nate had described this scenario. This was a raider group, a thing that just started happening a few days earlier. There was panicked desperation everywhere, and some people took to wandering in search of random violence.

Barney and Nate were both employed by the Prime Ministry, and both had intimate knowledge of the various systems and designs of G Mauve. Barney more in the administrative and political arena, while Nate was the planet's principal engineer when he retired two years before. Barney was still working, up-to-the-minute. Nate had spent a lot of time tinkering with various personal projects over the years, and made some significant advancements in technology. Barney imagined that they were actually well behind where they would have been if still part of an array, because they'd missed the collective achievements. There were thousands of Nates, even just at Galactos. Surely in three hundred years they discovered all sorts of things. Nate, though, was undeniably brilliant and inventive.

Nobody, not even Nate, saw this coming. The whole planet had known for centuries that they were not going to be able to perform the millennium maintenance. What they learned seven days ago was that not performing the maintenance was going to instantly shut down the entire ship. There were system reset subroutines that needed to check their box that the maintenance was performed prior to winter of the thousandth year. Those were set to trigger others, and so forth, with the result that in the absence of the maintenance bit check, the ship would shut down completely.

Nate, even though retired, still had plenty of interaction with the Ministry. One can't be principal engineer of a planet and just fade away. The subroutine issued a one-week warning that the maintenance had not been performed and the system would terminate, and they got Nate involved immediately. He was determined that there were ways to trick the subroutines, and he worked tirelessly with the engineering and software teams, but every avenue they tried reached the same point of processing and got kicked out. It didn't help that the code was a thousand years old and in a language that was only taught to specialists, because it was only for the ship systems and was a thousand years old.

In the end, Nate decided to spend this, the last day of autumn and the last day of ship power, on his porch, and

Barney needed to be there. Winter would begin with Earth's solstice, which that year was that day, at 6:04 p.m. and thirty-six seconds.

The force of gravity for a ship that size was certainly not negligible, but nowhere near that of a real planet, and the gravity they enjoyed on a routine basis was primarily synthetic and power-driven. No power, no gravity. If you remained motionless or just walked, you might stay put, but maybe a small jump would send you away for good. Regardless, the atmosphere, already assisted by a force field, would drift the same way. Cars and flashlights would still have lights as long as the batteries lasted, but only so you could see everyone dying for a few seconds. Indoors, you could retain both heat and air for perhaps a few minutes longer, but everyone freezes or suffocates really pretty quickly.

One of the things driving the situational madness of groups like the one coming down the street was that the news came too late to do anything about it, including helping people kill themselves. It was common knowledge that most people planned to commit suicide when the time came, and there was a scramble for things like drugs or other helpers.

Barney and Nate both had a single-dose, injectable poison pen. Poke it anywhere and push the button, and the spring-loaded mechanism shoots the stuff under your skin. Painlessly dead in seconds. Only the rich or the connected had those, and these two men were both. Most people did not have tidy options, and the frustration of anticipating any available death tipped some over the edge. Some even claimed they thought they were offering a service. A reasonably quick

—albeit violent—death. If only they'd kept it voluntary, Barney might have allowed them some slack.

The group of rowdies came further down the road, and Barney's head-up display gave an alert at four hundred feet. Barney was there largely because they were friends, of course, but also because he knew Nate was up to something, and that it involved raider gangs, but Nate had been cryptic about details.

"How close are they going to come?" said Barney.

"Close," said Nate, "but only because I let them. They get very excited when they get close. But they stay in the yard. I won't let them on the porch."

"How?" said Barney. "This has to be a force field of some kind, doesn't it?"

"Yes. But completely configurable."

"What?"

"Size, position, real-time movement, everything," said Nate. "See those boxes in the corner?"

Nate was gesturing toward the ends of the porch, which was about thirty feet long and ten feet deep, with a two-foot wall around all but the center eight feet, where the steps down to the front walk were. Above the wall was open air, with four stout pillars holding up the roof, which was a balcony upstairs. Barney did see wooden cubes in the two front corners of the porch wall, only a foot tall.

"Yup," said Barney.

"And out across the road. Can you see two grey rocks that look the same? The size of these boxes?"

From the porch steps, the concrete front walk went straight out ten paces to the sidewalk, but Nate's was the first house there, so the sidewalk only went to the right from Nate's walk. To the left, just grass to the road. Across the road was a band of grass, a bicycle path, and the river, but the band of grass sloped down toward the water, so from Nate's porch, one typically only saw the road, a tiny slice of green, and water. That day, abandoned cars further obscured the view.

"I think I only see one," said Barney, "but whatever. Emitters?"

"Right again," said Nate. "Specially modified through years of research, of course."

"Obviously."

"It's the same field as the atmospheric field," said Nate, "but configurable, and mobile in real time. I can create a number of shapes, and set the density from fairly permeable to absolutely impenetrable. No transfer of material of any kind, no sound, nothing."

Despite making logical conclusions about what Nate was describing, Barney was nevertheless astonished at this achievement. A real-time, configurable force field was speculated about from time to time, but Barney had no idea that Nate's little hobby project over the years was a functioning mobile field. This was revolutionary, breakthrough technology, and heartbreaking as well, with the immediate realization that even the array probably never developed this, and it was about to be entombed in a floating ice cube in space for potentially millions if not billions of years.

"Nate, are you serious?"

"As a genocidal subroutine."

Barney couldn't help but feel excitement ramping up quickly as the proximity of the gang was getting increasingly uncomfortable, but now the thrill of seeing a demonstration of this force field made everything electric. He took a quick sip of his drink, as if to steady his nerves, as he leaned forward slightly with a creak in his chair.

"Don't get up," said Nate. "It's not easy to stay entirely calm when they're here firing guns at you and stuff, and if you're up and about, I don't want any accidents."

"I wasn't," said Barney, "but I won't."

"Sounds good. Oh, here we go."

A couple members of the gang clearly spotted the two men, and began rushing faster down the road.

"How big is this field?" said Barney. "Can they go around it?"

"No, no, no," said Nate, holding the remote and moving controls. "Watch this."

Barney's head-up display gave the proximity warnings as the crowd ran the last few hundred feet toward Nate's house. A tall, blond man was at the front, wielding an axe, but just behind were two more men, dark-haired, one with a machete, one with two pistols strapped to his torso.

They came up into the yard at full speed, yelling and raising weapons. It was quite unnerving, and Barney found it very difficult to stay convinced he needn't move.

In the next moment, though, when the ruffians were still at least ten feet from the porch, the blond ploughed headlong into an invisible wall, making a crunching thud. The two dark-haired men were much too close behind him to react, and they also smashed into the force field and caromed off wildly.

The rest pulled up in bewilderment as the first three

writhed in pain in the grass. The first one had a fair amount of blood on his face.

"What the fuck?" said one of the women, an athletic brunette toting a large, complicated rifle.

A short, agitated man in a camouflage vest moved forward with his hand up, quickly making contact with the force field. "The fuck?"

"What the hell is this, old man?" said the brunette, at Nate. It was entirely possible one or more of these people knew who Nate was, or at least that he lived there. Nate was there a very long time.

"Some necessary protection, I'd say," said Nate.

Camouflage Vest was also armed with a pair of pistols, which he produced from holsters and pointed at Nate. "Well, protect this." He fired both guns, and the bullets ricocheted immediately off the field and away. He had to point up some to fire at Nate, so the bullets were just up in the air and gone. "What the fuck?" was the phrase of the hour.

"You will not be able to come any closer," said Nate. "Or shoot anything at us."

"Let's just fuckin' see," said the brunette, readying her rifle toward the porch. She let fly a spray of bullets, all zinging away immediately in front of her.

Several of the group instinctively flinched. "Holy shit," said Camouflage Vest.

The dark-haired man with the pistols, who had rammed into the force field, was working off the jolt and getting to his feet. "What is that, a force field?"

"Yes it is," said Nate.

"Seriously?" said the man. "A force field at your house?"

"Seems to come in handy," said Nate.

"Seems to be illegal as fuck," said the man.

"Can't argue there," said Nate, "but that's hardly relevant at the moment."

The man stepped forward with a raised hand and felt for the field, then pushed on its surface a few times. "Let's go," he said, turning away. The Brunette flipped Nate off.

There were additional gestures and obscenities, but the dejected group began to make their way down Nate's front walk toward the road. Near the road, they turned to go down the road into town, but abruptly jolted to a stop again. A few quickly turned back toward the house.

Nate called out to them. "You have to go across the street to get around!"

Angry and additionally frustrated, the gang made their way between cars, pounding on them and smashing a few windows and lights, and got to the grass on the other side.

"If they get around," said Barney, "can't they just come back across?"

"Watch," said Nate. He had flipped up a small screen on his remote now, and was performing some more precise controls.

The gang appeared to continue carousing, but Barney could no longer hear anything coming from them. He could only see from their waist up as they followed the force field wall toward the water, then stopped. It looked like they hit another wall, parallel to the river bank, and they became very agitated as they started to follow that one, now in the direction back where they were.

"Here it comes," said Nate.

"What?"

"Watch closely."

As Nate was saying that, Barney saw the brunette put her hands over her mouth and buckle like she was screaming violently, but he heard nothing. She pointed, and the rest of the gang made similar convulsions of shock and terror.

"There we go," said Nate, sounding like he just turned on a back massage.

Barney was altogether confused by this latest development. "What on earth is happening?"

"They found the bodies."

"The what?" said Barney.

"The other bodies. The other gangs. Hell, they can probably already smell them pretty badly, too, since I have the field on Solid. No air movement off the river."

"What? There are bodies down there?" Barney could scarcely believe what he was hearing.

"You bet. A half-dozen gangs like that. Murderous thugs."

Barney thought a moment. "How?"

"Air pressure," said Nate, utterly unfazed by discussing this. "When the field is on Solid, not even gasses breach, and I can make the box they're in very large or very small. If I make it large, then sweep to small, the pressure quickly kills people. Or I can go the other direction and kill them with vacuum. I like that option because I'm pretty sure all these people thought they'd escape that manner of death somehow."

Barney was silent for a moment.

"Don't even think about it," said Nate. "I know at first thought it seems wrong, but I got past that. I'm performing a service. Every single person I've killed out there committed

13

violent crimes. And we all die in a few hours. Just don't even pretend to lecture me. And don't pretend you don't know the magnitude of what I've done here."

Barney quickly thought that could be taken more than one way, but knew Nate meant the technology involved in manipulating a force field like that. And Nate was quite correct that Barney had to concede astonishment at this demonstration. But just then, Barney's head-up display showed HQ MESSAGE. His shirt had a chest pocket, from which he removed a small device with a screen. He plucked a stylus from its side and poked a couple times.

"Still not using vocal?" said Nate.

"For some things, I prefer pressing plastic to plastic," said Barney.

"So, what, reporting me to the Ministry?" said Nate. "Bureaucrat to the end."

"I am, but no," said Barney. "Message from them."

It was a distraction to try to read the message while also watching the local thugs clearly yelling and banging on the force field walls that kept them in a limited area across the street.

"Did you change their atmosphere?" said Barney.

"Not yet," said Nate. "Want me to?"

"Hang on," said Barney. "This is really, really amazing." He paused. "Nate, this is incredible."

"What? We aren't going to die?"

"No."

"Excuse me?" said Nate.

"Nate, they found it. You know how all the processing gets kicked out at the same spot? They found it. You won't believe this, but a zero got entered as an "O," and that screwed it up, because both characters were valid in that position. They just had different results."

"You don't say," said Nate, sounding decidedly unimpressed.

"Nate, they fixed it."

"Fix one, break another."

Barney was getting quickly tired of Nate's inferences. "What the hell are you talking about?"

"That's my code."

"No, no, this is buried in the original program subroutines."

"Mine," said Nate. "All mine."

Barney was excited to correct him. "No, it's not your fault."

"Ha! You're so cute."

"What do you mean?"

"Barney, my lad, I wrote it to do this."

"Wrote what?"

Nate paused, and it gave Barney a moment, one Nate was intentionally allowing him, to let his brain grasp what Nate had, in fact, done.

"Oh, my God," said Barney.

"Now you're getting it."

Barney was afraid to confirm, but knew he had to. "All of it?"

"All. There was never a reset program. Everything that has transpired this past week is entirely my creation."

Barney was slowing shaking his head in disbelief. Not disbelief that Nate had the skills to do this, but rather the motivation. "Why, Nate? Why do this? What good could possibly come from scaring an entire planet ship of people to their core?" He gestured toward the gang. "Were you trying to actually create this for some reason? Some social experiment?"

Nate paused, looking slightly bewildered. "Scaring?"

"Yes, that's what you've done here, Nate. Inflicted panic-stricken terror into everyone on G Mauve who thinks they die in about six hours."

"Well, they're going to get a surprise."

"Yes, but Nate, the damage this has caused. Why did you think this was necessary?"

"Can you imagine," said Nate, "the long, slow, agonizing deaths of millions over time as ship systems begin failing, one by one, and we can't fix them? No, Barney. I've prevented that suffering. No, this ship dies today, quickly and completely."

Barney was in new disbelief. "Wait, you mean…"

Nate laughed. "Oh my gosh! You thought when I said I wrote it, I meant as a joke!"

Barney's head was swimming in all this twisted information. "Nate. Answer me straight. The shut-down is real?"

"Real as the smell of those bodies out there. In fact, I'm curious that you had time to tell me about that zero-character fix."

Barney tried to latch onto the idea that they were back to where they started the day, knowing they die at the solstice. But now Nate was playing games about something else. "How do you mean?"

"Well, I wrote it. But I made it look like it hadn't been touched since the original coding. I'm guessing they'll assume the rest of what they think is thousand-year-old code is correct. And now they don't have time to check all the down-stream code, anyway. But either way, I'm a little surprised that they haven't reinitialized the reset program with that fix in there yet."

"How do you know they haven't?"

Their entire environment went completely dark.

"Because that's what it does," said Nate.

Barney heard the faint snap of a spring-loaded injection device, and reached into his shirt pocket for his.

MIKE ZIMMERMAN

Mike Zimmerman's returns for a second appearance in these pages after his fun "Splatterfairies" story last issue. Mike sent me this really fun story as part of the Pulphouse Fiction Magazine *Kickstarter stretch goal and it caught me right from the start, as I have a hunch all of Mike's stories will do.*

Mike is a full-time bestselling writer, editor, and brand storyteller who specializes in finding and honing a person/place/product's unique voice. He has done that across a multitude of divergent brands — from publicly-traded companies to national magazines to B2B mavens to household-name authors.

He uses journalism, research, analytics, good prose chops, razor-sharp copywriting, a bent brain, and a sense of humor to create world-class content for any audience. With far over 50 books in print, including 35 novels, you can find out more about Mike at zimwrites.com including information about his new book Jet Lag Is For Suckers.

THE AB

MIKE ZIMMERMAN

D wight Strine wanted abs.

    He hated how that sounded. The superficiality of it. Dwight found authenticity far more attractive as a creed and compass. He didn't want to acknowledge that he might be susceptible to the promise of a carved body, the lure of a magazine cover line or the salesy subtitle on a fitness book. *Four weeks to a flat, ripped stomach / the easy way to hard abs / 197 body-shredding exercises, one carved belly: YOURS.*

    Dwight was not the ideal candidate for abs and he knew it. Age 31, past his physical and hormonal prime into the stretch of years where booze and certain foods stuck to a man like ever-thickening coats of paint. Already 237 pounds on a five-ten frame. And this from an online trainer Dwight consulted: "Sorry to say, but not everyone can have abs." Giving reasons, because science.

    Dwight began anyway. He didn't want what he had. There had to be a better way. A better life.

Planks, hanging leg lifts, TRX pull ins, bicycle crunches.

Yeah, yeah, yeah, you trainers you. Dwight knew it was more about weight loss and body fat percentage than 500 crunches a day. He ignored the bent online stuff and went back to old magazines at the library.

your best summer body ever / get NFL tough / get results in 10 days / a six-pack plan for every man / fight fat and win

He'd already beaten the pustular psoriasis, he beat the super gonorrhea and depression, he was part of the intertwined knitted fabric of human destruction, he sure as hell could FIGHT FAT AND WIN.

Squats, box jumps, skater plyos, movements only the Russians, Romanians, and Turks knew, lunges in all directions because if you built the quads, the iliopsoas, the glutes, the biggest muscles in the body, your body will burn more burn.

Ten days later Dwight did not have abs.

But he now weighed 231.

You magnificent bastard.

———————

D wight never told anyone what he was doing.

He wasn't sure why his silence on the matter meant something to him, but it did. The authenticity again. What if pondering his physique counted as authenticity, what if daydreaming of a shredded torso and the admiration of others was part of an intentional life. But what if that was bullshit, his so-called values a lie? What if his pursuit of abs was all truly about who might notice, and when.

Yeah, that was probably it.

Probably, hell. He knew.

Dwight had to this point in his life been a nonfactor in the world. The proverbial cypher who offends no one and impresses even fewer. But he did examine his life on occasion and was not one to buy in on hype and appearances. He was not an early adopter because he was not a sucker. That's what he hung onto, what elevated him. He believed the ego, especially the male ego, should be silent, an invisible engine driving a man forward. Most men did not subscribe to that. So many strutters out there twirling their dicks, no, he couldn't be that kind of man. But this ... this he could do himself. A gift he could give himself.

Fitness and health and vitality and longevity, oh fuck yourself with all that, Dwight.

Admit you want to finally find out what's under the flab and flaccidity.

Man, that was exciting. He could finally find out. Who wouldn't want that?

That could be a new kind of authenticity.

Finding out lit a fire in him that had never been there before.

Do it. Find out.

———

"Look, not everyone can have a six-pack," the trainer said. He worked at the gym Dwight had joined. He was taller than Dwight, leaner, more broad-shouldered, and must have had a very hard time day-to-day not demanding all those around him to suck his cock. He looked Dwight in the eye with complete seriousness.

"Why would you discourage anyone?" Dwight asked.

Trainer smiled. "No, no, no, not discouraging you. Calibrating expectations. The whole six-pack thing is mostly genetics. Lookit me, even I would have to lean-down to a point that wouldn't be sustainable and even then, maybe. With your body you can get a strong, powerful core without a six-pack."

Dwight said nothing.

"I see you work," Trainer said. "You work hard. Let's do this thing."

Dwight walked away.

Abs or nothing and this piker wouldn't even try.

———

Dwight set to work. No timeline, just forward, every day. A lifetime spent in an unshaped, unkept, and unadmired body and now he embraced the push. It wasn't just that his daily workouts excited him and he couldn't wait to get to the gym. He felt the engagement of muscles in each rep and it felt … right. The mouthfeel of boiled skinless chicken felt right. The collagen peptides and creatine and chia seeds and oats in his smoothies felt right. The calorie deficit was electric in his belly, his metabolic center like an open mouth consuming his fat.

Squat jumps, Bulgarian body blasters, Garhammers, Spiderman lunges, deadlifts and dumbbells and death crawls.

He blew through 230, 225.

He followed a tip in one of the magazines about before-after photos. It aligned with his invisible ego-engine philosophy: He didn't take progress photos of his torso. He took pictures of his face. Dwight started with the puffy beer face, shaved his trendy beard so he could see himself. Really *see*.

This is me. But it ain't me, not really me, not just yet.

I'm in there and I will find my way out.

Everything he read about fitness and body transformation was true. Even the weeks when the scale didn't move, he felt his body changing. Something was always firming up and feeling different. He did stairs two at a time now. And his mind changed as well. His mind*set*.

new year new you change your body change your life

And the world still did not know what he was doing. He kept silent.

It was all for him.

66 six-pack strategies / firm up flab & sculpt a flatter belly / great abs made easy / muscle genius: the pro plan for ABsolute perfection

After two months, and the scale at 203, Dwight noticed the lump.

———

It was not an oh-my-God lump. It was a what-the-fuck lump. A protrusion at the upper right side of his belly, the very first ab if someone facing him started at the top counting left to right.

Dwight had already discovered the joys of what every male fitness enthusiast knew — getting to second base with yourself was irresistible. Heavy petting of your biceps, your glutes, your pecs, oh the pecs. Best tit you'll ever get your hands on because they're yours and *there*.

And so was the lump.

It was below the layer of remaining flab, subcutaneous, not inside him. And it was firm. A protruding knob of muscle. And very hard to unsee.

It did not stop Dwight. But it … occupied him. His hands regularly roamed over his changing body in true affection until they came to his lump. And his hands stopped. An unripe peach, a rubber ball, a knot of mockery.

Down to 197. Still there. Always there.

Fucker.

An imperfection in his perfect progress.

————

"I t's muscle," his doctor said. "Not even technically a malformation. Just … different."

Dwight held it in and only said, "I finally got myself … moving, right? I'm busting my ass for this."

Doc nodded. "It's remarkable, Dwight. You're the opposite of all my patients. But aesthetic perfection is a crapshoot. Hundred to one. A gift from the gods. A genetic lottery ticket. A freak chance at immortality. Of women, hundreds, thousands of women putting their hands and mouths on you. Men, too."

But the doctor stopped at the word crapshoot didn't he?

"Can I have it removed?"

Doc scowled, silence, then said, "I won't recommend anything when nothing is wrong."

What he didn't say was there were doctors who would see the enormity of his deformity. Who would do something about it.

"Dwight, you're letting one small thing get in the way of what's already a major victory. Forty pounds down, in great shape."

"It's unfair," he said.

Doc shrugged. "Not everyone can have abs, Dwight. And fewer people can have perfection. Take the win."

At 189, Dwight could see some torso definition in the mirror when he flexed. Not there yet. His selfie face was slimmer but neutral.

But the other thing was always there.

By now he'd accepted that this intruding thing was one of his rectus abdominis muscles. An ab among abs. Protruding enough to have its own shadow.

The rest of his body ... how to describe a dream? Dwight now looked, dare he say it, hot. His traps and connective neck and shoulder tissue flexed when he moved, his arms had grown bulgy and veiny, his pecs jumpy. He now saw more of his cock in the shower than ever before. He never skipped leg day.

And yet, unfinished. Still around 14 percent body fat.

Planks, jumping jacks, frog tucks, barbell rollouts, kettle-bell halos, medball chops.

fire up your fat burners / reshape your body in minutes / ignite your metabolism & burn fat all day / your best body EVER

He rubbed the ab more than he rubbed the rest of himself now.

––––––––

"Know what I think?" Fogerty said. Fogerty always said that because he always said what he thought, and he always liked people to know that. Dwight had known him a while but had spoken to him more often since they were both at the gym so much. Fogerty was a freak. He called himself a powerbuilder, some combination in his own mind of power-lifter and bodybuilder. He was doing the opposite of what Dwight was doing, trying to expand, enlarge, engrave his physique. Ever bigger and overblasted. He weighed 252 pounds, five-nine, could bench 440 but not do more than six pull-ups. Fogerty allowed himself straight vodka at certain times like now.

"How many times you hear someone say not everyone can have abs?" Fogerty asked, squeezing a rubber ball with his non-vodka hand as he paced.

"Every day," Dwight replied. He was buzzing fine, a plea-sure allowance he knew he'd have to work off later even though his progress really wasn't being set back by the liquid.

"Don't it piss you off people saying you can't have something?"

"Yeah."

"Know how I do this?" Fogerty replied, gesturing to his own physique. Then he pointed at Dwight's face. "Know what it takes to get abs for those who are not supposed to have them?"

Fogerty leaned and pointed. "Rage, motherfucker."

Leaned and pointed. "Nihilism. Misanthropy. Contempt. Your entire interaction with the world hasta change. An end of the self as you know it."

"Because no one really wants to execute. People just want to yearn."

"You want my advice about that fucking ab? Make it bigger."

"Lean the fuck in."

"Tattoo it."

"Name it."

"Because fuck it. Fuck the ab. Fuck the world, Dwight. I'd take a fuckin' bat to the world if I could. The world and guys like us no longer deserve each other. So fuck it, Dwight. Don't hide it. Make 'em see it."

———

Down to 180. 12 percent body fat. His abs were evident but not yet shredded.

Women noticed him now. A few did, anyway. Only one was hot. They locked eyes once their eyes were finished with the rest of themselves. Nothing happened, she passed by.

If anything had remained locked up in Dwight, that moment with that woman unlocked the rest.

He invaded social media. He walked taller. He presented himself.

At the gym, Dwight performed his ever-deepening ballet. He thought of the slo-mo dancing in *Raging Bull*, that music, the boxing dance, the physical god, the poetry, the sweet motion in motion in motion, look at me, archetype, godlike and then ... someone would see him and the music would stop. Because he was not that. Not yet. Strip away more. *It's in there. There's more in there we can't see yet.*

His tight workout shirts showcased the ab. He swam shirtless in the gym pool.

And they looked at it. Before they looked at him.

score the six-pack you've always wanted: more than 100 core exercises / lose your belly fast: 10 gut-busting 15-minute workouts / attack the fat

ATTACK THE FAT

My God it's happening. It's working. I'm doing what no one else can. I'm becoming what almost nobody is.

Why don't more people do this?

Because they can't!

———

172 pounds. 9 percent body fat.

The outer fringes of shredded. Gorgeous. "You could do porn," someone said in the gym shower.

Dwight was close now. Crossing the 170 mark and he could stop and assess, measure, see where he really and truly was not just physically but in his soul. Was he still authentic?

Could he achieve authenticity with his new body? He was fast approaching the summit of the least conquered peak in modern human existence: Human male perfection. He achieved it all by himself ... and he was deformed.

Sometimes Dwight woke in the morning knowing the ab had been whispering to him all through the night. Glorifying itself and telling him more more more there's always more. And inside its tone was the teardown, Dwight, you're unworthy.

The ab was an atrocity. Without it, Dwight would be perfect, sporting the ideal six-pack. The combo of grief and rage made a shit stew in him. It wasn't fair. He'd done what he was supposed to do, paid those very specific and expensive dues, what hardly any people have been able to do. And the whole thing was an abortion.

Always there. The ab.

The cosmetic surgeon turned him down. The man had a six pack himself, but a sloppy sick looking one created surgically from lipo and etching because not everyone can get a six-pack. He wouldn't remove the ab or mess with it in any way, *this is muscle, not like taking out a calcium deposit or fat and I can't predict what the outcome will be. I don't mess with muscle, you see.*

And Dwight knew the ab had spoken to the doctor. The doctor palpated it over and over, measured it, did everything but apply his mouth to it. The ab mesmerized now. It charmed. What is that, lookit that body, what is that?

When Dwight laid down on his bed his belly was a hard undulating expanse of stone and the ab was a temple rising from the desert, Uluru, Devils' Tower, and they all came to worship now.

The man in the gym sauna, *that ab is amazing, lookit it*, he touched it, *how do you get it to pop like that, I'm dying for that pop*. Dwight and the man weren't caught.

The woman at the nightclub with her manicured hand under his shirt rubbing it rubbing rubbing rubbing trying to grip it tongue in his ear moaning on the dance floor.

The shirt came off and another woman pressed into him so she could feel it against her.

Shirtlessness, another goal achieved, god-level shirtlessness.

———

Dwight got a promotion at work, more client-facing opportunities and he had all-night sex with an intern after drinks. She claimed she'd never experienced anything like it and lookit it, lookit it, *why can't I stop touching it*.

Most mornings now Dwight woke with people in his bed.

The ab was red and shiny from being rubbed and palpated and loved.

Dwight selfied his face again and saw a sad clown carved from bone.

He worked out shirtless at the gym so they could all watch even though the rules on shirtlessness were clear. No one dared tell him to put a shirt on. Trainer watched closely but kept his distance, humiliated and denied his part in Dwight's glory.

Bicycle crunches and mountain climbers and burpies til you belch, sleds til you puke. Shadowboxing with dumbbells, rucking around the building with a 30-pound plate in his pack and a kettlebell hanging from each fist.

That Instatrainer's page still claimed not everyone can have abs, repeat not everyone can have abs and Dwight left his screed in the comments: BUT I CAN!!!

Dwight searched out new techniques. He found a physical therapy cycle for low back pain even though he didn't have any, a crumpled piece of paper discarded on the gym floor, and he tried the little movements, high reps, 160 reps in less than 10 minutes. Miraculous. His new warmup. His core a machine, 25-pound med balls slammed and side-tossed against the wall and hurled upwards over his head and off the gym ceiling.

He dabbled in average rate of methylation change and epigenetics and his microbiome and he dreamed of energy harvesting from human batteries.

And finally, Dwight broke his one rule. He posted an after photo of his physique.

Because now he must.

The comments came fast.

The very first: "Lookit that ab!"

"Five-pack and a tallboy!"

"What the fuck is that! No, seriously WTF IS THAT!"

"You so abby, you abby someone, abby NORMAL."

"freak"

"ugly"

"put a shotgun under your chin"

Dwight hit refresh and refresh and refresh again.

But then … a night wore on and another night and his local fans invaded the comments and overwhelmed the haters.

"glorious"

"an inspiration"

"orgasmic"

With one graf in particular from SheGetSheGetSheGetHIGH: "I know this man. I have been with this man. I have seen what he's become and he is a walking mission statement. He works harder than any of you. He loves harder than any of you. And he WAS you. He decided being like you wasn't good enough and he changed. And look what he found. Lookit that beautiful perfect thing on his torso. It is everything. It is him. And I will never get over it."

Definitive.

Yeah, that was the one. Definitive.

———

A muscle magazine found Dwight. Saw you on social, please let us interview and photograph you. You did it, man, you made yourself. You're the best story we've ever heard and everyone will learn from you.

One day Dwight was naked with a woman in her apartment and she presented him with a shirt. *I made this.* Snug over his muscles, the shirt had a hole just for the ab, the hole the center of a swirling tie-dyed maelstrom with embroidered crystals and glyphs and when he asked her what they meant she said, "You will decide," and fellated him.

Dwight knew the ab was a lump of muscle but pictured it full of pus and bean gas and one day it would pop in some lover's face.

———

F ogerty dripped some vodka as he declared.

"You are the One, that thing and you make the One." Dwight could hear the capital O in Fogerty's voice.

"The intertwined, knitted fabric of human destruction," said Fogerty, pacing, pointing. "Everything, our economy, our need, our hope, our society rests on obsessions like you."

"You are finally at the border where conclusions stop mattering and beliefs take over."

"You don't need conclusions anymore. You are a brand ambassador for achievement. A god of men."

Fogerty slugged down vodka, he hadn't been at the gym as much anymore, he wasn't peak powerbuilder anymore. "That thing, that fucking thing in your center, it's your magnet, Dwight. Who needs a compass when you have a magnet. Everything comes to you."

———

D wight accepted an invitation to attend a queer underground art rave where he stood nude on a platform while below him dozens of men stripped down to leather straps and codpieces and easels and brushes painting their impressions of him and the ab. Later Dwight fell into them in darkened rooms and deafening music. The following night the paintings were shown at a nearby gallery and he attended in a black blazer and jeans and no shirt. The woman who owned the gallery told him, "You and your thing are the thing."

Split-stance cable chops and medball rotations and dumb-bell seated twists and stability ball reaching crunches and three rounds on the canvas heavy bag, bare fists and torn knuckles.

great abs made easy / blast fat in just 10 minutes / top 5 flat-belly foods

He spent a weekend in an apartment with four female roommates going bed to bed being naked with them and he held the hair of one of them as she puked and he let the ab touch her bare skin while she hung over the toilet. She started laughing when she felt it. It was all okay. Everything he did was okay.

Dwight starved himself and carved himself, shedding calo-ries, shedding empty food, selecting only nutritionally dense mouthfuls, and if he could have, he would have hand-wrapped each protein molecule in its own spinach leaf.

He went to his doctor more to show off than anything else. Doc said to him, "You're down to 165, don't lose another pound."

"Look at me," Dwight said.

"I am. You have to see the mirror, not just the scale."

"What's my blood say?"

"You're healthy. Technically."

"Then I'm healthy. I've made peace with my deformity. Look at it."

———————

A Hollywood producer, the guy who made *Romper* and *Stomper* and *Chomper*, wanted to Zoom. *Maybe there's something*, he said. *Saw you in the magazine, saw your Insta. You're so imperfect you're perfect. Maybe you're an anti-hero, anti-establishment, untouchable. Unconquerable. And not a whiff of CGI. I think you'll be fucking loved. Yeah*, he said. *Maybe there's something.*

Dwight received death threats from men who wanted to cut off the ab and sell it. A man from Kansas City wanted to eat it. Rumor had it the cosmetic surgeon who turned Dwight down had created a solid silicone implant the same dimensions as the ab; three successful surgeries so far. Dwight received pleading notes from others on how to do what he did. Why can't they have the ab? He did podcasts and more interviews. He put his name on a ghostwritten foreword to the 10th anniversary reissue of *The Men's Health Big Book of Abs*. A 17-year-old boy hung himself from the side of a high school because he couldn't get abs like the ab. Dwight's employer gave him a leave of absence at full salary for as long as he needed to do what he needed to do. But come back, they said. Your job will always be here, they said. (And with many interns, his boss whispered in his ear, hand gripping Dwight's elbow.)

And Dwight realized he was there, finally there.

He now lived with complete authenticity. With complete intentionality. Everything he did he'd considered first: *Is this me?* The ab guided him, brought him love and touching and money.

He told people he thought about pushing his life even further, what else was within reach *cuz my grasp is longer and stronger than I ever thought. If I can do this what else can I do?*

But inside he had no other ideas or plans.

Dwight was perfect but he was not okay. And never would be because none of us can be. Like the special shirt with the hole that woman made, the ab rose up and pushed through the intertwined, knitted fabric of human destruction. And Dwight knew he could never truly live up to the ab's promise. The fraud collapsed in on him.

He whispered into his attorney's ear as they spooned naked one morning. "It's a lie, I'm a lie, I hate it, it's a fucking deformity, I can't stand how I look, I just wanted abs, I just wanted—"

And the attorney scrambled away from him to the other side of the bed. "They will kill you if you say it. I will kill you if you say it again. You can't. You can't, Dwight. I have never felt something shatter my cynicism so utterly, do you understand me? I was unreachable and look at me now! That thing is every blessing incarnate. Even if you aren't."

She composed herself and slid back over to his side and touched him and said, "It is you now."

whittle your waist / a sexy, sculpted stomach in just 4 weeks / lean hard abs that can take a punch

———

Three days later, Dwight skipped leg day.

"Haven't seen you at the gym," he said to Fogerty while sipping a heavy beer containing more calories than his breakfast. It might as well have been a milkshake. Fogerty had switched from vodka. The big man was no longer as big. Dwight didn't ask but he estimated Fogerty at 233 now and deflated.

"I'm off the needle, I need a break, it's just not sustainable, I want to enjoy my life," Fogerty said among other things. And then he said, "I can't have what you have."

Dwight put his beer down. "Hell, *I* couldn't have what I have and now I have it."

Fogerty waved at the air like the words could be flicked. "I know so much more than I used to know and what I know is the world's given us a sweet taste for sour shit. We're all just eating shit, Dwight."

The big guy winked. "But you keep going, man, it's important probably."

———

Blistering day on Manhattan's west side. Shards of sun off the Hudson as Dwight stood on a platform. Before him on the flight deck of the U.S.S. Intrepid stood more than a thousand spandex-clad people waiting for the music to start, waiting for Dwight to lead them. He'd never led anything. All he had was his setlist, a list of exercises he would cycle through, increasing stages of intensity for one hour. Seven cameras and two drones. A total-body workout class *en masse* with he and the ab guiding them all. He'd gotten the invitation to be flown in and do this live on social for a silly amount of money. His first time in New York.

He tried to do what the books suggested, be present, be in

the moment, but all he could think was *not everything needs to be meaningful, not everything must be a growth opportunity, why can't some things just suck, I can't even be good at feeling bad* and the music began and his hosts barked happily into their headsets and everyone moved in glorious unison, high knee footsteps stomping on the tarmac and soon they all glistened in the sun. Dwight forced his smile and sincerity and he felt like he was making simultaneous eye contact with all of them. All staring at him through their breathing and smearing sweat and bouncing bodies.

And then they chanted.

Over the music, to the beat: *Lose the shirt lose the shirt lose the shirt.*

His hosts beamed at Dwight, nudged, gestured, and he pulled the sweaty shirt off careful not to yank his mike and battery. They saw it and they cheered. One of his hosts roared with joy and approval as he reached in and rubbed the ab.

The workout played on, the eye contact the smiles the panting, and Dwight saw each rivulet of sweat pouring off every single person, gallons of it, lickable, it could feed him, quench him, he could drink it til he puked, til he blossomed.

And as he saw the jubilation in their faces he also saw the savagery. The threat underneath. They could so easily reach out for him but not to touch the ab, to peel his flesh and pull his heart loose and eat it all and curse his fucking name because his flesh has no flavor because it has no fat.

Only then would they cut the ab free. Release it finally and leave him behind.

He must never stop. None of it can ever stop. The Intrepid

workout may have been his best ever. He flexed and gyrated and took them to heights. Every new moment a new orgy.

The ab gleamed over its smaller abs in the summer sun.

———————

D wight continued to walk through his new life. But he didn't speak as much. He marched along and surveyed everyone he met like he did in New York, seeing their need and their deprivation and their inability. It occurred to him, that no, he couldn't burn it all down. Not now. But the ability to burn it all down, to destroy all their dreams, was a beautiful new bulge — on his ass because he kept this in his back pocket like a detonator. When it came time to destroy their world, he had the weapon. His fraud, his misery, his deformity, his dismissal of ever-deepening every-second growth, and his syphoning of their riches into himself to feed the ab. He had to admit it was unique. He had to admit it was power. He had to admit that his beautiful, attached, depraved and desperate attorney had been correct that morning. To tell the truth was to destroy. And it would give them all reasons to kill him right back. Having that power was new nourishment and allowed him to see the reality of his world.

Maybe he could find good. Or at least savor the bad. For a while.

Dwight stopped skipping leg day. He went back to the religion of the gym and practiced like a pope. The producer promised a story meeting very soon. A New York editor he met on the Intrepid offered him a six-figure book deal while still sticky in his hotel bed. He slept with five new lovers this past week, women and men. He moisturized the ab twice daily and the ab remained shiny and red and abominable and abdominal and the thing they all really wanted.

Dwight understood their want.

Everyone can be fitter stronger faster better. But not everyone can have the ab.

ADAM-TROY CASTRO

For this month's featured story, I could try to describe it and fail. I think there might be only one writer on the planet with the ability to pull off this story and that is Adam-Troy Castro. Just the way his mind works and he has the writing skills. Stunning. Might be the most Pulphouse story ever in these pages.

Adam is a seasoned professional writer who sold me and Kris stories in the very first incarnations of the different Pulphouse magazines back in the late 1980s and early 1990s.

This is Adam's fourth appearance in this new incarnation. You can find a lot more information about Adam-Troy's work and his amazing and long career at his web site adamtroycastro.com.

RUBBER DUCK

ADAM-TROY CASTRO

I am aware of where I seem to be and what I seem to be doing, but I refuse to believe it.

This is one of the privileges I am afforded as a sentient and enlightened inhabitant of a rational universe. I can assess my surroundings. I can determine that I happen to be immersed in a luxurious steaming bubble bath, at just the right side of the pain threshold, that it is not cooling and that I am flushed from the heat; and that I happen to be clutching a lilac-scented bar of soap fresh enough to still bear the sculpted logo of the brand that it seems to be, my face tingling in the flushed manner that it tends to, when I am still adjusting to the temperature.

Okay. So I am taking a bath. Big deal.

Rub-a-dub-dub.

Further details, of which there are many, some suggesting delusional insanity:

My knees are little islands rising from the foam, being

lapped at by the ripples caused by my every movement, and at the other end of this claw-footed basin there is a spout with twin dials to regulate the temperature, though that seems to be constant and so does the water level, which is not slowly escaping from the drain the way bathwater does whenever there's an imperfect seal.

The air that brushes the exposed surfaces of my skin is foggy with ambient warmth, a steamy balm that feels good as it enters my lungs; and all that is as vivid and tangible as the idiotic rubber duck that bobs between my knees, a permanent wide-eyed idiocy stamped on its face.

I must say that this is the platonic ideal of hot bubble baths, a favorite indulgence to which I have treated myself, not quite daily or even weekly but often enough, over the years. It is as perfect as any bubble bath can be, warm and comforting and ridiculous in all the right measures, and the temptation is to do what these sensations have traditionally urged me to do, which is to say turn off my relentlessly logical mind and surrender to peace.

Okay?

But I am also aware that I am in outer space, that the claw-footed receptacle that contains what I am forced to consider a contained atmosphere is, just out of reach, frigid and deadly and focused on that task the space between planets is always focused on, snuffing out the life of any being who happens to be floating unprotected in this starry immensity.

I know the dimensions of what I guess I must call the bubble because the vapor rising from my water rises only about a man's height above my head before it encounters the threshold between the atmosphere within and the vacuum without. It seems to collect against that invisible membrane, not enough to block my view of the surrounding stars, but enough to present a semblance of atmospheric turbulence that blurs the rest of the universe before escaping into the endless void.

When I first found myself in this impossible place, hours or days ago, I worried about the permeability of this bubble, fearing that what air I had to breathe would escape soon and leave me to asphyxiate where I grow pruny; but it has been a long time without any degradation of the atmosphere, days, and so I have had to accept that the unknown architect of my predicament, perhaps God, has engineered the water, or perhaps the bath, to keep the nitrogen/oxygen mix constant. I am not in danger of anoxia or of carbon dioxide buikdup. But I am in a bathtub between the planets and perhaps between the stars, and all this, all this, in the name of heaven, without mentioning the alien yet.

I will get around to mentioning the alien. I must. He is just outside my bubble, matching speeds as he races alongside me and tries to get my attention. He is quite insistent. I must get to him, but I am not quite ready, as my mind has reached its capacity just analyzing the implications of the tub. He is somewhat human, this alien, though a caricature of humanity, and his body language seems to indicate urgency, so I must sooner or later accept the impossibility that contains me and broaden my scope to accept this representative of another world who is gesturing for my attention, at a distance so minimal that were this a real bathroom I could roll my eyes, step dripping onto my bath mat, and cross the room to determine what the invader wants. One of the things that has kept me from doing so is the awareness that even if he's real and not some hallucination, I cannot hear any of the vital, urgent things he's saying and that therefore there must be hard vacuum between us, despite the negligible distance; and that therefore if I took one step out of that tub and stepped heedlessly into the emptiness I would not be able to benefit from his input into my situation. My eyes would bug out, my lungs would deflate, the sheen of bubbly water on my skin would freeze and boil simultaneously, and I would have time to consider just how stupid I was, just how much of a dumbass I would have just demonstrated myself to be in the face of a survival situation that some legitimate science fiction hero would have figured out and handled with aplomb long ago. It is not my fault that I am not Spock, nor the Doctor, nor the brilliant Andrea Cort of those novels I read years ago. I just know that I cannot deal with the alien now and that I do not want to think about him. Let him gesture. I can feel and sense that this is really happening, but I am not yet ready to think about it.

I shift positions, not by much but to satisfy my body's hunger for movement. That's another thing. It is the only kind of hunger I feel. I know that my stomach should be growling and that the back of my throat must be raspy from lack of water, and my normal biological process should have befouled my bathwater long ago. That would have been unpleasant. I have feared it coming but it has not come. Either my sense of time is off, or I have not been abandoned to this place without some kind of adjustment to my metabolism, to prevent the evacuation of bladder or bowels and the pollution of my medium. I suppose I should be grateful that whoever or whatever put me in this bath, with snakes – and I will describe the snakes soon -- without seeing to my long-term comfort; certainly, given the physics that I know regulate the reaction of human skin to warm bathwater, I should be grateful that the delicious comforting warmth that one feels after first immersing itself in liquid of this apparent temperature has not faded to mere wetness as my skin adjusted to the differential. These are good things.

But there are other things that have been neglected.

For instance, there has been no provision for emotional or intellectual stimulation. Back home in my regular life, a thing that I know must have existed but of which I can summon only the vaguest personal memories, I sometimes slipped into a warm tub with a paperback book in my one dry hand. I turned the pages with my thumb and enjoyed the plot while, myself, being an inhabitant of the pot that boiled. Sometimes I would read entire chapters that way. In my home the toilet was within reach of the tub and, when I had enough, I could place my current volume pages down on the lid, my place in the narrative thus assured as I used my toes to replenish heat, and lay back, my eyes closing as I surrendered to naptime. I have once or twice in my life stumbled into mentioning some book I read in the bathtub and been surprised into the reaction of whoever I was speaking to that this was deeply abnormal behavior, an eccentricity to be scorned even more than the perversion, in some eyes, of reading books at all. Who the hell takes a book into the bathtub with them, they wanted to know. What was wrong with me? I cited it as just something to do during my quiet time; and here, surrounded by infinite space and the sound of the waves lapping against the sides of my vessel, is nothing but quiet time. They should have given me a book. Or a book reader. And possibly loaded a bloody explanation. That would have been nice. Instead, they gave me a rubber duck, a bar of soap, and an alien in a state of panic.

That's not nearly enough to occupy my mind, at a time like this.

———————————

There are two aliens now.

I did not see the second one arrive. I was engaged in not paying attention: not the wool-gathering, not-bothering to engage, sort of not paying attention, but the kind that involves active effort, like a child clapping hands over her ears and screeching, *La la la, I can't HEAR you,* while her big brother's trying to bother her with a gross joke kind of not paying attention, the kind that takes effort, the kind that involves obeying the command to, for god's sake, whatever you do, not think of an elephant.

Have you ever done that, not think of an elephant? It seems a simple instruction. Just don't think of an elephant. But then your mind, girding itself, responds with, *what exactly am I not trying to think of, again?* And you, seeking only to help out, picture an elephant, either a plush stuffed-toy kind of elephant or some creature from a nature documentary, standing in the middle of open savannah, being an elephant. "Oh," you think, annoyed now, because you really were trying to not think of an elephant, "don't do that again," and your traitorous inner voice responds with, *Do what again?* And before long that inner voice provides you with enough elephant to repopulate the grasslands, from noble bull elephants protecting the herd from attacking lions, to old-fashioned circus performers riding oversized tricycles around a ring, to King Babar of the books I know about but have never read, to political cartoons about the Republican Party, to old pulp illustrations of that story about Conan the Barbarian trying to burgle "The Tower of the Elephant," and so on, culminating with images that picture elephants engaging in activities no elephant ever has or ever should attempt, one leading to the next as your compulsive gray sponge spits out more elephants than any being, including horny elephants, could ever want. It is impossible to consciously not think of an elephant. Your imagination cannot help itself.

And it's especially difficult now, given that the alien that has joined the first one racing beside my runaway space-faring bathtub, damnably happens to be an elephant.

I don't think I can avoid this issue any longer. I'm not quite ready to think of or *not think of* the elephant keeping up to my bathtub on the right, but if this situation is just going to start piling up the impossibilities to some point of truly infinite absurdity, I need to address it and start actively looking fr a logical explanation.

So.

To summarize, I've been taking a bubble bath in deep space. I am breathing within some kind of contained atmosphere, in what seems to be hot water, though it never gets any colder and I never grow accustomed to its temperature due to my skin ultimately matching the temperature of the surrounding medium. I know that this one detail is unlikely to the point of near-impossibility and so I take special care to note it, because it's hard data and I need such hard data to come up with some explanation that mighty conceivably include me being delirious or insane.

To my right, at about twice the distance that my old toilet was, back when I used to use it the bath-adjacent table where I used to put down my paperback books, is an elephant, chasing after me with the gait that real elephants use while charging, though to my knowledge no elephant has ever charged through interplanetary space in pursuit of a bathtub.

I will *not* think of that.

Damn it. I just did.

To my left, also pacing me, is the first alien I saw, the one who's been keeping up with me since the beginning.

I specify that *alien* is a provisional explanation, the best I can do given my current limited capacity for acquiring data. I mean that I have no more information to go on than at the very beginning: that it was weird-looking and that I did not want to think about any more than I want to think of the --

Damn it again. Damn it all to hell.

Forget the elephant.

To my left is a green-skinned little man riding in the cabin of a cartoon red locomotive. By *cartoon* I mean that it is clearly animated, not just in the sense that it is in motion, but in that it appears to be a drawing, with simplified lines and detail work that includes two crossed white bandages on its chassis. What distinguishes it from a traditional terrestrial locomotive, let alone a cartoon one, is that its fore and aft sections are attached to rollers that are laying down track ahead and collecting it again, behind. The vehicle simulates the usual locomotive in that it therefore rides on tracks, though I am at a loss to justify such an arrangement being necessary where there's no planetary surface that the rails need to be laid on. I have plenty of other reasonable design questions why the machinery has been set up this way, but that is another mental pathway that I can get lost on at distressing length and I will not allow it to occupy me, any more than I will think of the elephant. *DAMN IT.*

The locomotive has a smokestack that once every, it seems to be, five seconds or so, inflates with internal pressure and relieves itself with a puff of smoke. Although such smoke would dissipate quickly in a planetary atmosphere and even more quickly in vacuum the little puffs of smoke do not; they recede into the black distance and remain visible for a long time, useful in that, with a backdrop consisting of distant stars and absolutely no landscape they provide ample evidence of our forward movement. There is also on the roof of the cab a protruding whistle that gets excited, in a cartoonish way, at the same rate that the smokestack produces its clouds, and though there is vacuum between us and I cannot hear it I would bet any amount of money, if I had any, that it is at this intervals going, *Whoot! Whoot!*

(Do you see why I was not ready to actively think of this?)

Elephant.

God *damn* you, already. Leave my head alone.

The creature I think of an alien is holding on the open threshold of the cab and doing whatever he can on heaven and Earth to get my attention. He is shouting, waving his free hand, even jumping up and down a little, out of his urgent need for me to respond. He is wearing one of those old-fashioned blue-striped engineer outfits, including the cap, and whatever he has to say is urgent indeed, though the silence of vacuum means that he should either save his breath or find some place where breath is possible. He is human enough for me to read his expression, which is just the wrong side of panic. I ae called him an alien and not an engineer because he appears to be a distant cousin of the big almond-eyed grays of UFO-cultist lore: no nose, no lips, and oversized eyes of the sort that, together, have always made the visiting aliens of popular folklore look like knockoffs of a human fetus. What he can be yelling, what he must want me to do, is beyond my imagination. But there's lots of pointing involved. Every few seconds he jabs his oversized index finger at, I guess, my knees. The alternative, that he's pointing at that private part of me that remains obscured by mountains of glistening white bubbles, is too risible to be borne: I mean, is he upset that I'm naked and taking a bath in what an alien engineer at the controls of a space-traveling cartoon locomotive might presume to be "in public"? *Fine*, I want to reply. *Throw me a towel.* And that prompts an entire series of unprofitable thoughts about how one would go about catching a towel that, tossed the short distance between his locomotive cand the bubble that contains me, would be briefly exposed to hard vacuum. Would it freeze? Burn? Absorb enough radiation to kill me? I don't possess the scientific knowledge I would need to formulate the answer, and all of this is irrelevant anyway because he's *not offering a towel* and I don't think it's what he's trying to say anyway.

Then I realize that he's changed strategies.

Aware that I cannot hear him and that the challenge of imparting entire sentences is beyond my ability to lip-read, he's changed his strategy. Now he's just yelling the same word, over and over, at what I would presume to be the top of his lungs, if lungs are indeed relevant to his alien anatomy. Determining the precise word is not an insoluble problem. It is a word I have seen other people mouth, from time to time, usually when they wanted to assault me from a distance. I presume that I have not consistently been offensive enough to invite it, but nobody speaking English is wholly free of exposure to this worst profane words, or of indictment for on occasion using them. He's shouting this word, the F curse, over and over, with vehement extra emphasis now that he can see I recognize it. And this, alas, provides absolutely no clarity. So a cartoon alien – a clown, really -- in a shiny red locomotive wants to make anatomical suggestions. Maybe he wants to make a right turn and I refuse to get out of his way. Maybe he hates the human race on mere principle. Maybe there's some cultural imperative understood by members of his ancient and noble species, that I have violated out of ignorance or cultural insensitivity, that would never understand because of the evolutionary gulf between us, and that even if an explanation was offered would sound like gibberish to me: an accusation, for instance, that I violated his *Grifnil* on the Holy Day of *Yogsponk*. Maybe he's just a belligerent ass. Who knows? But there he is, shouting *the* word with as much vehemence as he can, as if could possibly provide the answer to anything at all. Shouting back mighty be the answer, but if he is hostile I don't want to be hostile back. This is no time to provoke an interstellar war.

So I watch him fulminate for a while, offering no reply but silence, and after a while he gives up and collapses against the edge of the threshold, and damned if he doesn't weep. A message has been sent, for some purpose incomprehensible to me, but no useful information has been received. He is frustrated. He is bereft. He is mourning his own failure to communicate. Part of me wants to tell him that it is his own fault for using bad language, and that is the part that makes me contemplate the nature of this failure, the bad language that is not just bad because it should never be uttered in a respectable place like church but because it fails to convey meaning. I find that I do not believe he was trying to abuse me at all. He had something very vital, very critical, to impart to me, something that he believed fully contained in his choice of word, but which I could not decode because I was alien to him and operating from a different set of assumptions. To believe otherwise is to believe the universe meaningless, and I will not do that even now, trapped in this place. Not even doing what I'm doing.

Not even remembering the elephant.

I nteresting. A new element has been added.

There is a certain frustration attendant to this: to wit, there is already so much I cannot explain that the addition of yet another element is intensely frustrating. I know that supplemental detail helps resolve puzzles, but everything so far has seemed so random that this just new thing seems like another nonsensical detail to confound me.

It is a paperback book.

It only makes sense here because, as I've noted, I long made a habit of reading in the bath, and while here I bemoaned the absence of a book to occupy me while I lay here with pruning fingers. But I cannot read this because this particular book has been encased in some kind of indestructible plastic that my fingernails cannot tear asunder.

It appears to be a thriller, packaged as horrific science fiction. It's called *Submerged Through the Void*. The author is one *C. May Tarr IV* and the cover image is of myself in my current situation, submerged chest-deep in an old-fashioned claw-foot tub, racing with abandon through interstellar space. I get the title and after some cogitation I also see that C. May Tarr IV, a name that for me evokes some author you would find in the earliest science fiction pulps, is a tortured almost-homophone for *See Metaphor*, which to me indicates that it's at least trying to pointing me in the direction of a clue while not giving me one. The metaphor doesn't seem to be the locomotive piloted by the clown, which isn't on the cover and, I guess, outside the range of the instruction. There's no elephant either, which is especially irritating, which means that is also outside the range of the advisory, but is annoying anyway, because it makes me think of the elephant. *See Metaphor.* Is the elephant supposed to indicate that those old-school politicians, the Republicans, are somehow to blame for my problems? I doubt it. I seem to remember that both the major American political parties of my youth, the Republicans and the Democrats, are gone, swept away when the shifting demographics of the time reorganized both into different coalitions, with new names that I've known all my adult life,but which remain fuzzy to me, lost in the memories I can't access. And besides, there are no elephants on the book cover, anyway. Just me in my tub, soggy between the planets, perhaps between the stars; the reality I am supposed to focus on, that the book wants me to know.

There is a review quote, in italics, beneath the title. It reads, *"A Thrilling Race Against Time, and a Hero who must gather the courage to see it! –* Kirkus Reviews." So, okay: the wispy, clouded nebula that provides the backdrop for that runaway bathtub is a clever phantasm, resolving after much examination into a screaming human face, a larger version of the face of the hapless figure in the bathtub. The close-up is key. I am supposed to recognize that face. In the context of the pictured bubble bath I make the cognitive leap that the face must be mine, even though I still don't know who I am and the features are unfamiliar to me. The smaller image of myself is dozing. I place my thumb over the somnolent face and I can discern a definite vibration, generated by the book cover and carried through the plastic covering and the skin of my thumb. I cannot hear the sound it is making but I capture the rhythm of its song and perceive it as snoring.

So, okay, the guy in the tub, the version of me, is asleep, so persuasively so this portrait of me has been equipped with its own snore, which is definitely a new experiment in published.

It is not a gigantic leap to discern that whoever sent this book wants me to know I'm asleep, which would by itself be a welcome explanation for my nonsensical situation, but the major problem with taking it literally is that I happen to know that I am awake. I have already performed some basic experiments to confirm consciousness. I happen to know that you cannot feel pain in a dream. You can endure the conviction that you're hurt, as in a dream I can summon from a childhood I otherwise remember only in errant fragments, of being cut in two by a guillotine blade dropping from the sky to cut me in half. In the dream my top half was separated from my bottom half, and so my eye had to regard my sundered legs from a distance, and tell me that I was feeling untold agonies from the separation. But I did not then, and have never, felt any real pain in any dream where I was wounded. I just knew that the pain was there. I *posited* pain, as an abstraction, though while asleep and watching these little mind-movies never possessed the wherewithal to know the difference. And this is importance because here in the tub I have been able to pinch the loose skin on the back of my hand with the grasping fingers of another and have been able to inflict enough pain to feel it. I have placed a soapy thumb between my teeth and bitten down hard, stopping only when my only options were to stop or scream, and that was definitively pain: definitely what would wake me up if I were asleep and churning the fantasies that come with sleep. So I'm not dreaming. I am awake and actually *either* spending the long interplanetary or perhaps even interstellar afternoon in a bathtub or *only thinking I am,* which would indicate a powerful perception problem, I guess.

I'm a hundred percent certain that I am on to something.

I glance at the book cover and find that the illustration has changed. Now it's a different image, that of the same naked man adrift in a golden void, being menaced on all sides by snakes. They are cobras, all of them, converging on him from the boundaries of the frame. The author is the same, *C. May*

Tarr IV, and the top review quote is now *"...like all the devils of Hell were on his trail"* – Kirkus Reviews, and there's now a breathless line of publisher-written copy, *With time running out for all humanity, will he see the truth before it's too late?* I get the impression that somebody's screaming in my ear while trying to slap me awake. But I am awake – I mean, I once again test that postulate with a cruel pinch – and so it's not a question of waking up, not exactly. It's a question of finding the epiphany, of realizing.

Of understanding I am refusing to see.

I feel the truth just beyond the reach of these wrinkled fingertips. It's something terrible, I know. I am aware of a terrible danger, threatening death or worse, and it takes everything I have to not shtug this all off, to not retreat to the warmth of this womb-like bath and embrace the soporific effects of the hot, steaming water.

Womb-like.

That means something. I'm sure of it.

A bathtub. A clown riding a locomotive. A bathtub. A bar of soap. A paperback book. Snakes. An elephant. Is that all one metaphor? Or many?

What am I missing?

I'm missing the soap.

Where's the soap?

It was floating before.

Why can't I find the soap?

Why is it so important that I find the soap?

Why do I suddenly feel cold inside, in a way that is not ameliorated by the steamy warmth of my surrounding atmosphere?

Help me.
Please help me.

I'm running out of time. I can tell because the chill inside me now definitely feels like a shutting-down from the inside-out, a sense of whatever powers me gradually fading away: a decline. I don't need to see everything around me as it really is to know that it means I am dying and that the only way not to die is to find a path to understanding. I still haven't found the soap, but I know that it is critical; as critical, or approximately as critical, as the shrink-wrapped paperback, which again has changed covers, with the same author and this time a title indicating a philosophical treatise, *The Key To Life and Death.* The illustration is a bleached human skull on what appears to be an African plain; the review quote is, *"Tell all your friends!"* – *Kirkus.* These new details provide me with no epiphanies, but they reek of immediate danger. I feel that if I manage to resolve this into anything concrete I will feel stupid for not getting it until now, but I can take what will no doubt be a public humiliation. It'll be better than death.

The back of my throat burns. I remember being trapped, somewhere, in some place on fire. It is the aftermath of some terrible event, and the air around me is all billowing black clouds. I want to scream, but the air is scalding. My lungs rage from my insult, and my throat, my poor throat, feels like I just swallowed a fistful of razor blades and washed it down with pure acid. I remember being aware that I have just seared my lungs and having the warm, comforting knowledge that this means I will suffocate in less than a minute. I know I am dead, and from the point of view of what I know to be years later that before this happens I will be retrieved and frozen in cryo and sentenced to more life and that I will not take this as a blessing.

You can't feel pain in a dream. But you can't feel it in memory either. You can only remember the way you once reacted to it, not how you felt in full sensory detail, but how it felt to feel it, the overwhelming sensation that of how it *felt* to feel it. How it was so frightening, so overwhelming, that when you think it's about to happen again your mind retreats inside denial, inside a *metaphor*.

A hiding place can be as comfortable as a warm bath.

It can be so comfortable you never want to get out, even if the whole universe outside you is screaming at you to wake up.

The title of the book has changed.

It's now called, *Just Look.*

But at what?\

For some time I descend into despair. This is hell. This is nonsense. This is madness that no human being can figure out. And the worst part of it all is that it is ludicrous. The= worst thing Hell can be is ludicrous. Yes, it's even worse than painful. Imagine a hell where you are pummeled by soft pillows for all eternity. No, it does not hurt. No, it will never hurt. But it's all there is, all there ever will be, for centuries and millennia and eons, and there comes a time when every soft thwap is like another chisel to the brain.

Why can't I get out of the bath? Why is there nothing but the bath?

I don't even have the consolation of feeling clean. A bath only cleans if you then use a shower to rinse, and there is no shower here. You ever smell your own face? I smell my own face. I have been sweating down my cheeks for days or weeks now, and though I've occasionally wiped them there is still accumulated salt, and it smells funky. Were it not for the book continuing to assure me that I am running out of time, and all of humanity with me, I would presume this to be a permanent condition, like that hypothetical eternal beating with pillows; to always have a smelly face.

I am also aware that all this self-pity is unseemly.

I glance to my left, where the locomotive is still keeping pace. The clownish cartoon engineer is still framed in the doorway, but he is no longer gesticulating at me. He's just floating there, blank-faced, reacting to me the way anyone reacts to a fixed feature of his landscape. I could wave back, I suppose, but what's the point? He cannot communicate with me and I cannot communicate with him. Maybe he's as tired of this existence as I am. Maybe he despairs over the failure of meaning as much as I do.

And meanwhile my goddamn face still smells.

What happens next is a pure, self-loathing impulse, something that should have happened before but which profound ennui over my situation has prevented until now.

I shift and sink my head under the surface of the water.

I don't know. Maybe I just want to drown myself.

But in that instant everything changes.

What I see I have been seeing all along, but misinterpreting on the edges of drug-induced hypersleep.

It is not bathwater because it is not water.

The liquid has a light golden tint, uncomfortably close to that of urine. It appears carbonated, or at least like it releases gas for some other reason. Wherever I look, bubbles the size of pinpricks rise upward, gathering against the ceiling of this sealed chamber, where an angled surface urges them toward the exit ports where they are collected and recycled. The liquid itself is thicker than ordinary water, enough to cushion me against acceleration or sudden changes of course, as it would be, because this is not a bathtub but a travel pod, which actually is traveling through the interstellar gulf, as pictured.

Of course, there is no bubble of captured atmosphere above this liquid. There is just a ceiling, against which the bubbles pool and gather before being forced out those recycling ports. I was never head-and-shoulders above the surface of a bubble bath, though I was looking at the air trapped against my ceiling and seeing an atmosphere instead of the liquid I'm breathing.

This is what I have been forced to look at, what my twilight consciousness to explain with a fractured metaphor. My mind didn't want me to be here, so it picked elements from my immediate environment and altered them to their more mundane equivalents, with more, like the elephant and some other things I have not figured out yet, forced into their own bizarre alternatives just to fit inside this image.

So: the snakes. They are the tubes that feed me, some of which feed me and dose me with various necessary medications while others carry away my wastes. They pierce my chest and my belly and there are two up my nose and I have a catheter and I have another thicket of flexible cords measuring this and that to make certain that the subject, myself, is being properly maintained.

I understand that this is where I have always been, all this time, and further I realize what this place is called. It's a goldgel crypt, an environment where I am meant to dream in timeless slumber, while I travel the distance between a destroyed homeworld and a destination chosen for resettlement. It is a bath, all right; just not one meant for luxuriating in hot water. Something has obviously gone wrong with the mix, hence my consciousness. I am between consciousness and sleep, my sense of time supercharged, my mind experiencing a moment of borderline wakefulness as the days I have thought I was traveling space in a bathtub.

My right hand still grips what I thought was a bar of soap. It is a little white object attached to my palm and it is indeed about the size of a bar of soap, and for a moment I perceive it as an old-fashioned black telephone, complete with rotary dial. I only see that because my mind, still trying to explain it, has conjured it, and my mind has only conjured it because it is one element of antiquated technology I happen to know about, being a man with some basic interest in vintage artifacts like paperback books. The image is the best my mind can offer as explanation for why this object exists and what I'm supposed to do with it. But it must be a faulty metaphor, because even as I watch the black telephone fades away and the bar of soap returns, for some reason a closer analog to its true purpose. I have not figured this out yet but I can come back to it.

More to the point are the screens inset in the capsule walls to my left and right. They are designed to feed me information during moments of partial or even full waking. The one to my left is a view of what I imagined to be a cartoon locomotive. It is another pod like mine, mounted on a metallic strut, connected to mine by another strut, and backed by thousands of other pods just like it, bunched like grapes against a branching superstructure that stretches as far as the eyes can see.

Or not eyes; the image is after all a real-time video, providing a helpful image of the pod next to mine, as if that's information I'm supposed to find useful when I'm vegetating in the next closest thing to sleep.

The space between my pod and that one is obscured by a haze of debris that includes a frozen human hand, severed from the form of the cartoon locomotive engineer. He is not alien and not a clown, but he might as well be, as he's dead. Whatever happened to this pod has ruptured it, and the force of all that exploding liquid has carried his body to the threshold of the fresh opening, exposing him to the vacuum between us. He is caught where he is because he is still teth-ered in place by some of the wires and tubes meant to service his health while he lay in place, pruning. He does appear to be looking ay me, but this, I understand, is an illusion; his eyes are as open as his mouth, but he's looking at nothing, as he will continue looking at nothing, forever. His constant furious wave is the product of a hand that cannot drift away to find its own destination, because by chance one of the more delicate tubes piercing his skin at the wrist remains intact, anchoring it in the gulf between us, anchoring the hand palm-out, almost as if it's trying to get my attention.

I swallow the knowledge that in my semiconscious stupor I have been staring at a corpse on a screen and interpreting it in the most fatuous manner possible, because my mind would not accept what I actually beheld.

I can track my thoughts now. They are slow, drugged, and sludgy. I remember my name and I remember how I got here, how we have all gotten here, how we were all told were about to be unceremoniously evicted from the planet and how we built this ark, this survival mechanism for getting us to some-where the survival of the species might be possible. Stupid details from the last few desperate years insist on intruding, and I wave them away, because they are not as important as what the images my mind dredged up were trying to tell me, most pressingly with the various covers of that paperback book. Clearly, whatever happened the pod next to mine, whether some kind of random collision with debris, or an actual attack by something sentient, was catastrophic; just as clearly, it remains a danger to me and everyone still traveling with me. Maybe everyone there is, period.

But I am trapped inside my pod. That I am alive, at all, is testimony that I am still within an airtight seal; that the fate of the man to my left testifies that even a complete rupture of this vessel will not allow me to escape it and take whatever concrete action might be possible, with nothing but my own volition, is also clear. I am not a captain. I am not a member of the crew. If either of those things exist, whether alive auto-mated, I am not capable of acting to that extent. I am just a poor slob who, lying in his pool of piss-colored murk, happened to realize that something had gone wrong and happened to muster enough consciousness to, distantly, understand it. What did I think I could do? What could I amagine I could do?

I begin to wish that I'd remained asleep, or if that was not possible that I'd remained within the irritating whimsy of the claw-foot tub and the cartoon alien engineer. Oblivion may not be productive, after all, but it's comforting, to someone who can do nothing. Even if he dies he can die in peace, spared the knowledge of local disaster, or imminent personal extinction. He can enjoy the gift of not knowing, of believing himself fine, of believing the apocalypse an abstraction, far away and not intersecting his orbit in the slightest. If I could return to that and leave the problem to be solved by someone else, I might consider it – but I never would, because I can sense now that it runs counter to who I am.

There always was something womblike about bathtubs.

I glance at the rectangular object attached to my palm, the one I'd imagined a bar of soap, and then briefly, before it changed back, into an old-fashioned black telephone. Why was it those two things, in particular? Am I expected to clean up this situation? Is that the idiocy I'm being told? Is it the telephone that I'm supposed to pay attention to, instead? I am stuck by what may connect a bar of soap and a telephone, especially such an antiquated telephone. The answer eludes me. It is in the place inhabited by the grand idea I have just before I fall asleep, that retreats behind fog and no longer exists when I wake. I have the idea that it will remain obscure for as long as the connection eludes me. I probe at it, and hammer it, and fail to force the available data into the hard action I need. The answer seems like it would be simple, like it must be simple, and yet it still seems absurdly complicated, too obscured beneath my veil of fog.

So all right, where's the rubber duck?

What is the rubber duck?

It was something that existed as a constant inside the metaphor, and I cannot find it. I am aware, by now, that it cannot be literally a rubber duck. There is no reason except for whimsy to bring a rubber duck aboard a space-ark to a new world. I sense and reason that whimsy of that sort was in short supply when the crisis came. I can find no free-floating object, anywhere around me, that would be translate ta rubber duck in a bathtub. Its absence frustrates the hell out of me. What is it about a rubber duck? That it squeaks? Possibly. But there is no object around here that squeaks. There is no unaccounted-for object at all. I wonder if the rubber duck was not a symbol, but an unexamined association, something that just goes along with the premise of a bathtub – corroborative detail, if you will, something that came up not because it served the metaphor only because it was something I expected, like a saddle on a horse. But no. Now that I have started to decode this, I can feel its significance.

I ask myself what practical purpose a rubber duck serves in a bathtub.

The answer comes rolling in: none.

But no artifact exists without purpose.

Unless it's…art?

No.

It's whimsy.

A rubber duck is a toy. A rubber duck is a little floating object that mimics a cute personality, to share a bathtub with you. For an adult, it's nostalgia for childhood. For a child, it's company.

And what service does that company serve?

I get the answer:

Reassurance.

If you are a child, you are afraid. It is your default reaction to the unknown. Of course, childhood also means bravado it also means considering yourself indestructible. But you also live with fear built into you, a useful default to retreat to before you learn to distinguish the unknown from the genuinely dangerous. You have other things like that: a soft plushie animal, a flannel blanket, a favorite nursery rhyme that for you boils down to the comforting lie that there is nothing here that can hurt you. A rubber duck is physical manifestation of that promise. When I thought I was in a bathtub, it was a natural conjuration, a reassurance that everything was going to be all right. And now it is gone. I am aware that I am in danger. I know that the rubber duck is a false promise.

So, okay. I know what the bathtub is. I know what the snakes are. I know what the cartoon locomotive is. I know who the cartoon engineer is.

I do not yet know what the soap / telephone is.

And there is something still addressed, something that I now realize is the most important thing in this entire scenario.

The elephant in the room, the thing I have been so obsessed with not thinking about ot.

For the first time in I don't know how long I check out the monitor to my right.

The object dismantling the pods on the struts in that direction looks enough like an actual elephant that I am in addition to my natural horror bitterly disappointed with myself for conjuring such a facile metaphor. It has a machine, not an animal. It has a thick gray body, a vast head with a central manipulative tentacle, and two sharp and narrow protrusions that it is currently using to rip its way inyo a pod near me, to get at the meaty corpsicle inside. The space behind it is rich with debris torn from pods like it, and empty pods reduced to empty shells now that the human beings inside them have been torn loose. There must be hundreds of the destroyed and thus hundreds of the dead: and part of my display is a numeric counting down the number of the living, as they are eliminated one by one. There are, I can see, still millions, though there is an another associated numeric that establishes how many tens of thousands are gone. There is a count of the invaders: hundreds of them, enough to slaughter al of us in no time at all. There is no way of telling whether the pachyderm-adjacent invaders are manned – or aliened – by living things like pirates interested in mining us for canned food, or mechanisms warring against us because of their programming, but they are here and they are ravenous and we will not survive long against them, if we do not activate some kind of defenses.

I want to scream.

But there is still the soap, that is sometimes a telephone, to account for.

Why would there be monitors inside a pod where I am meant to sleep my journey? For the same reason I have that object affixed to my mind. Because there have always been unexpected dangers, and there might well come a time when one of the sleeping must wake, summon consciousness, and take definitive action. Artificial intelligence might do the job, but there come times when whatever threatens us is nothing artificial intelligence can recognize or be programmed for. There comes a time when human senses can see, when it takes a human mind to react to an imminent threat.

The final puzzle piece snaps into place. This is a generation ship, with a large fraction of the human population asleep, a much smaller population servicing the needs of the whole. Armed, I presume. Just not aware. They need someone to tell them.

I only needed the command to initiate communication.

The object attached to my palm is neither an old-fashioned telephone or a bar of soap. But the two artifacts had a single word in word, and even as the armored marauders converge on my position, I form that word in my suddenly fully conscious, fully remembering mind and blast the message through that connection the people who might come in time to save us.

Dial.

ANNIE REED

Professional writer Annie Reed writes stories that span genres and are always powerful. In fact with Annie, you just never know the type of story you might be reading, but you will always know it will grab you and be a compelling read.

Just the title of this story is fun, and the story goes from there.

So far Annie has had a story in every issue of this magazine and as the editor, I hope to continue that streak.

Annie's stories have appeared in four best mystery stories of the year volumes so far. Look for so much more of Annie's work at her website anniereed.wordpress.com.

THROW THE ZOMBIE FROM THE TRAIN

ANNIE REED

T om Cruise is a god.

I don't say that from personal experience. He could be a jerk or the nicest person in the world, how would I know? But the dude hung off the outside of a *speeding train* for one of those *Mission Impossible* movies. Hung his ass out there with his clothes whipping all around him, wind hitting him in the face like he was standing out in the middle of a hurricane or a wind tunnel or the wing of a jet—which he actually did for another movie—and the whole time he stayed in character like a damn rock star.

Movie magic, you say? Yeah, maybe, but I'm kinda thinking not, since my girlfriend read me some headline a while ago about how he did his own motorcycle stunts and even got hurt doing one once. Or maybe more than once. When she gets talking about celebrity gossip and all the stuff she sees on TikTok and Instagram, I kind of tune her out.

Especially if there's a *Walking Dead* marathon on AMC. The early years. The new stuff's getting a little too weird for me.

Like I should talk, right?

Here I am, hanging on for dear life to the *outside* of a speeding train without the benefit of ropes or wires or any of those harnesses they make actors wear to make sure they don't actually die on set. All because I decided to cosplay a zombie.

I'm not even the only guy dressed as a zombie on this train. But no, the dickheads I caught tearing through my luggage must have somehow decided *I'm* the zombie they're after.

I don't know what the hell they were looking for. One minute I'm walking down the passageway to the room—excuse me, *roomette*—I'm sharing with my best bud Wolfer so I can touch up my makeup, feeling pretty good about myself because some cute zombie girl said she liked my costume—hey, just because I've got a girlfriend back home doesn't mean I can't appreciate a cute girl when she crosses my path—and the next I find these two goons in our roomette ripping up the place.

"Hey!" I said in my best outraged twenty-two-year-old voice. "What the hell?"

That's when one of them grabbed me by my moldy, dirty, blood-stained shirt—zombies don't do laundromats—and slammed me up against the outside wall.

The one with the picture window I'd admired when I first boarded the train.

The one with Emergency Exit stenciled in red between the two panes of the window.

"Where is it?" he screamed in my face. "C'mon, zombie. Spill!"

"Where's... what?"

Goon One was about ten years older than me and had a good sixty pounds of muscle on me. He had on a dark suit—no blood or guts hanging off it—and his face was flushed as red as a semi-ripe tomato. He could have been cosplaying a villain from one of those early James Bond movies for all I knew.

"It's not here," Good Two said as he threw my duffel bag on the floor. "Must be one of the other zombies."

"Great." Goon One actually gritted his teeth. I could *hear* them grinding as the muscles in his jaw flexed. "What're we gonna do now? He's seen us."

"No, no I haven't," I said. "I can't remember anyone to save my life." That wasn't exactly true, but hey, when you're faced with imminent death and bad dialogue, you'll say pretty much anything.

The next thing I knew, I heard breaking glass, and then Goon One picked me up like I weighed nothing—and okay, I'm not exactly a bodybuilder and I am pretty skinny, but still —and hefted me *out* the broken window!

I don't know how I managed it, but I caught the window frame with one hand, which was the only reason I didn't plummet down the very, very, *very* deep canyon alongside the train.

I half expected one of the goons to smash my fingers to make me let go of the window—that's what villains always do in the movies—but they must have decided I'd be dead meat in short order anyway. I would have been too if I hadn't managed to bring my other arm up so I could hold onto the window with both hands.

That was the best I could do. I tried to pull myself up, but it was a total failure. I just wasn't strong enough. Plus I was shivering my ass off.

It was the middle of October and the train had been climbing into snow-covered mountains for the last half hour. Icy wind was slamming into me and cutting right through my zombie costume. (Zombies also don't wear coats, stupid zombies.) I don't know how fast the train was going, but as far I was concerned, it had to be at least a hundred miles an hour.

I made a promise to myself that if I got out of this alive, I'd start doing pushups and pullups and all that other upper body strength stuff I'd totally ignored since high school P.E. classes. You know, just in case something like this ever happens to me again.

So here I am, dangling off the side of a train, trying not to look down while I'm wondering how much longer I can do this since my fingers are already going numb. And you know what I'm thinking?

Besides wondering why the hell Tom Cruise voluntarily does stuff like this to himself?

I'm thinking that this is the last time I let Wolfer talk me into going on a vacation like this ever again.

———

"C 'mon," Wolfer said. "It'll be a blast, man! Non-stop party. Lots of fangirls. We can dress up like zombies and everything."

We were lounging on the couch in the apartment I share with my girlfriend. *The Walking Dead* was playing in the background on TV—one of the early episodes when both of the redneck Dixon brothers, Daryl and Merle, were still alive. Wolfer had been thumbing through one of the social media apps on his phone while he devoured a family-size bag of Cheetos.

Up until a minute ago I'd been playing a mindless game on my own phone. It was Saturday afternoon, and Beth, my girlfriend, was off doing some girly thing with her friends, so Wolfer and I had decided to hang out. I'd just about leveled up on my game when Wolfer texted me a link to a website advertising something called The Unwalker Experience—a *Walking Dead* fan con party train.

"Hey!" he said. "We can even dress up like Daryl and Merle. Wouldn't that be a hoot?"

He was really into the idea. I can always tell. We've been buddies since eighth grade. By that time, *The Walking Dead* had already been on the air for a few years, and it was Wolfer's absolute favorite show. We were too old to go trick-or-treating and too nerdy to be invited to any Halloween parties, but that didn't stop Wolfer from buying a cheap Halloween costume knockoff of Daryl Dixon's signature leather vest with the angel wings on the back.

Wolfer's dragged me along to a few fan cons, mostly local stuff that's geared more toward anime or comics, but the party train was different. One of the major national con promoters was in charge, for one, so it probably wouldn't be lame. Then there was the swag—exclusive *Walking Dead* memorabilia, the website promised. But the real draw was the private screening.

The party train was scheduled to leave Sacramento at ten on a Saturday morning and arrive in Reno some six hours later. Party goers would get a few hours free time to wander around the casinos, for those old enough, or grab something to eat at one of the buffets before going to a private screening of two early episodes of the show in a casino showroom.

The thing that really got Wolfer's attention though was the live, in-person commentary for the episodes by the director and two of the stars of the show. Afterwards, the fans would get a chance to party with the stars at the casino until the con-goers headed back to the train for the return trip to Sacramento.

24 Hours of Fun! the website promised.

And below that, *Cosplay encouraged!*

And below *that—Register early! Space is limited!*

"What do you say, you and me?" Wolfer said. "I mean, Beth won't want to go with, will she?"

Beth? On a cosplay train with a bunch of *Walking Dead* fans?

"No way," I said. I love my girlfriend, but her idea of a good time was a day spent trying on clothes she couldn't afford to buy, followed by treating herself to boba tea and mochi-nuts as a consolation prize.

I noticed the link didn't mention *which* stars would be doing the commentary. Not that it would matter to Wolfer.

His big ambition was to meet as many stars as he could by the time he was thirty. To that end, he'd convinced me to stand in long lines at other cons to get autographs from guest actors who'd appeared on one episode of a television show that went off the air ten years before we were born. Although one old guy who'd been in *The Rocky Horror Picture Show* had been signing tighty-whities, and that had been kind of fun.

If Wolfer really wanted to go on this trip, and it looked like he did, I could just tell Beth is was our mini-vacation for this year.

Beth calls our out-of-town trips "boys' night out," but it's really just something we started doing a couple of years ago to blow off steam. Wolfer works in the warehouse for a pet food manufacturing company. My job's just as mind-numbing as his, only I'm stuck at a desk making collection calls all day for a medical supply company. The trips out of town, usually a weekend in San Francisco where we'd go to a pro football game and then bum around down by the wharf, gave us both something to look forward to.

The train trip wouldn't be cheap, but it wouldn't be that much more than the cost of a couple of tickets for the nose-bleed seats to watch the 49ers get their ass handed to them by one of their West Coast rivals. Especially not if we shared a room on the train.

"I could probably get Beth to drop us off," I said.

Beth and I live in Davis, Wolfer in Woodland, not exactly next door to the train station in Sacramento. She was a night owl, so picking up Wolfer and getting both of us to Sacramento by ten on a Saturday morning was a pretty big ask. I could probably sweeten the ask by telling her she could get to the shops at Arden Fair mall early enough to beat the crowds. Plus her favorite mochi-nut shop in Sac was only about ten minutes from the train station.

"So we doing this?" Wolfer asked.

I had to admit it sounded like an actual fun fandom experience. Even if I had to dress up, which I hadn't done since the last time I went trick-or-treating in sixth grade.

I shrugged. "Sure," I said.

"Awright!" He high-fived me with a Cheeto-dust-covered hand. "Party time!"

We registered for the con that day and spent the next few weekends putting together our cosplay outfits. Instead of dressing up as just a plain old zombie, I decided to play Zombie Merle since I knew Wolfer wanted to cosplay as Merle's brother Daryl, his absolute favorite *Walking Dead* character.

Wolfer tried to convince me that if I wanted to be an authentic Zombie Merle, I needed the knife gauntlet thing Merle wore as a makeshift prosthetic after he cut off his own right hand. I said no way. Not only was my left hand practically useless, since I was strictly a right-handed man, but I was sure I'd skewer someone with the knife part. Even if I made the whole thing out of cardboard and duck tape.

As I clung to the window frame with both hands, I thought I'd made a pretty good call about the knife/hand thing. We might not win the costume contest as the Dixon brothers, but Zombie Merle never had to hang off a moving train.

"What the hell?"

I looked up to see Wolfer hanging his head out the window.

"What are you doing out there?" he yelled at me.

A million smartass remarks flew through my brain, but all I said was, "Pull me up, man!"

Wolfer's not a bodybuilder type either, but since he spends his days loading bags of pet food onto pallets for shipping, he has the kind of arm strength Thor only dreams about. Wolfer clamped onto my wrists, braced himself with one foot against the wall below the window, and heaved.

I tried to help out by scrabbling my feet against the slick side of the train, but really, it was all Wolfer. Several heart-stopping minutes later, he yanked me through the broken window and I flopped to the floor, only just managing not to hit my head on the door.

Our room's pretty damn small, have I mentioned that?

We opted for a private room, err *roomette*, so we could catch a few hours sleep on the trip back to Sac, and the only reason I even had a duffel bag was because I packed an extra cosplay shirt, complete with dirt and fake blood stains, along with a second set of clothes that would be comfortable enough to sleep in. Most of what had been in my duffel bag was zombie makeup, including my bottle of fake blood and the extra sets of latex face appliances and glue that I used to make my skin look like a zombie's.

My clothes were strewn around the room, but all of the zombie makeup was gone.

To quote Wolfer, what the hell?

I explained to Wolfer what had happened with the two goons. Who had apparently stopped to take my zombie makeup on their way out the door.

"We gotta tell somebody about this," Wolfer said.

I agreed. But what kind of a description was I going to give? That two Bond villains attacked me, threw me off the train, and stole my makeup?

Wolfer helped me to my feet and we took off in search of a con staffer.

The train had left Sacramento a couple of hours ago, and by this time the party part of the party was in full swing. Beyond the sleeper car which housed our very tiny room, a group of passenger cars had been converted to party central. Most of the con-goers we saw were in cosplay, from simple zombies to character zombies—I saw at least six other Zombie Merles, which made me wonder if any of *them* had been threatened by the Bond villains—to pretty damn good versions of Sheriff Rick Grimes and badass katana-wielding Michonne.

The party cars only had soda and bottled water available, but that hadn't stopped some of the partiers from bringing more potent beverages aboard. The aisles were wall to wall people, some of them definitely feeling no pain, and the theme from *The Walking Dead* was booming on repeat. At one point I got whacked in the head by a cosplaying Daryl's crossbow, which kinda hurt even though it looked like the crossbow had been made out of PVC pipe, thick cardboard, and lots of duct tape.

With all that mess, it took us a while to find a staffer, a thirty-something woman who looked totally overwhelmed. I didn't blame her. While we'd been waiting in line to board at the station in Sac, I'd heard another staffer say that the party train had sold out in less than a week, all five hundred seats.

Five hundred cosplaying zombies and *Walking Dead* characters. Reno wasn't going to know what hit it.

We got the staffer off to one side and I told her my story. It took three times, shouting to be heard over the din, before she got the gist of what had happened to me, and I had to take her back to our room and show her the broken window before she kinda believed me.

"You sure you just didn't break the window on accident?" she said. "You know, that waiver you signed makes you responsible for any damage you cause while you're on board."

She meant the little checkbox we had to click before our registrations went through. I hadn't read it, of course—who actually reads those things?—but it didn't matter because…

"I didn't do it," I said. "Goon Two did right before Goon One threw me out the window."

"Hey, look at this," Wolfer said.

He'd squished himself against the outside wall so all three of us could squeeze into the room. Which was freaking cold, what with the broken window. He was pointing to a bit of black cloth caught on a piece of glass hanging off the top of the window and blood on the frame next to it.

"That's not your blood, is it?" Wolfer asked me.

I shook my head. I'd been lucky. Well, as lucky as you can get when you're tossed through a broken window. At least I hadn't cut my hands on the glass. The glass on the bottom of the window was actually all gone, or else I probably couldn't have hung on for as long as I did, and the only blood on the rest of me was all fake.

Plus, the Zombie Merle shirt I wore over my blood-covered undershirt was more faded gray than black.

"So let me get this straight," the staffer said. "We're looking for a Bond villain with a bloody tear in his suitcoat." She took a deep breath. "On a train full of cosplayers covered in fake blood."

"But probably not a lot of Bond villain cosplayers," Wolfer said, no doubt trying to be helpful.

The staffer bit her lower lip. "I told corporate we needed more staffers on the train."

"Wait," Wolfer said. "Exactly how many staffers are there?"

She gave him a baleful look. "Three, plus two security guards. One in front, one in back."

"For five hundred people?" he said.

He shared a *you've got to be kidding me* look with me.

"It's a train, they told me," she said. "A closed environment, you know? All here to have a good time? The staffers in Reno will be riding back with us. Guess they figured everyone would behave on the way there and only get rowdy after the party tonight since there's not supposed to be any booze or weed on the train but who knows how many people will get drunk in Reno, so we'd need more staffers then. All I was supposed to do was check everybody in and make sure they got to the right rooms and seats."

She went on for a bit, wondering out loud which security guard she was supposed to report something like this to and what they could do about it, but I'd tuned her out.

Something was bothering me.

Something about looking for a Bond villain.

I'd really only gotten a good look at Goon One, the guy with the tomato-red face and grinding jaws. I had no idea what Goon Two had been wearing or even much what he looked like. He could have been anybody on the train, but I was pretty sure I'd recognize Goon One again.

Unless...

I grabbed all my clothes off the floor. Wolfer hadn't brought any extra clothes, just a coat that was still stuffed next to mine in a tiny compartment hidden behind the bench seat that turned into his bunk. The clothes I planned to sleep in after tonight's party, and after I removed all my zombie makeup, were all there.

But my extra zombie cosplay shirt was gone.

Along with my makeup.

Crap.

"We're not looking for a Bond villain," I said, holding my clothes in my fists.

"But you said..." the staffer began.

"My other shirt's gone," I said.

"Aw, crap," Wolfer said. "And all your makeup."

The staffer looked back and forth between the two of us. "What does that mean?"

"We're looking for a zombie," I said. "A red-faced, square-jawed, bodybuilder type zombie."

On a train full of five hundred *Walking Dead* cosplayers.

The staffer blinked at me. "Aw, crap," she said.

———

The three of us decided to track down the security guard stationed at the rear of the train behind the sleeper cars.

"He's probably the least busy right about now," she said, "since the party's going on up front."

Except for those who were partying *in* their rooms. One half-dressed zombie girl spilled out of one of the rooms, followed by a cosplaying Governor, complete with black shirt and black eye patch.

The staffer shot me a look. "That him?" she asked.

"No," I said. The Governor cosplayer was taller than Goon One, and he didn't have the square jaw I remembered.

"Oops!" the half-dressed zombie girl said when she caught sight of the staffer's neon yellow vest. "There's no rule against..." She waved one hand in the vague direction of the room's open door. "You know."

"Two consenting adults," the staffer said. "Just keep it inside the room, okay? And keep the drapes shut?"

The girl grabbed the Governor's hand, giggled her way back inside the room, and shut the door, pulling the drapes closed over the window in the door.

"Not exactly the mile-high club," Wolfer muttered, but I knew he was sort of jealous of cosplay Governor since he hoped to hook up with a fangirl on this trip himself. We'd even worked out a system in case he got lucky and needed the room to himself tonight.

"Actually," the staffer said as we kept walking toward the back of the train, "we're getting close to the summit and that is over a mile above sea level, so..."

"Not the same thing," Wolfer said.

The staffer and I shared a look. "Even a fanboy can dream," I said.

Before I'd boarded the train, all I knew about the inside of passenger trains was what I'd seen on television and in the movies. I'd expected a drafty, dangerous passageway between the cars, but really, other than the accordion-like folds in the walls that surrounded the connections, going from one car to the next was just a matter of opening two doors. I kind of lost track of how many cars we went through until we got to the last car in the back.

"What, no caboose?" Wolfer asked.

No, just a security guard in the last room in the back.

Sound asleep on the bench seat in a private roomette just like the one I shared with Wolfer.

Right down to the broken window.

———

"He's not asleep," Wolfer said. "Somebody knocked him out."

Wolfer had to take a first-aid class before he was cleared to work loading pet food pallets. Why, I don't know, but he's a good guy to have around if you choke on a piece of hot dog or need your pulse taken or, you know, need to bandage a head wound.

The security guard had a pretty good-sized bump on the back of his head. He was an older guy, probably in his fifties, with the name of a private security company embroidered over the breast pocket on his plus-size black shirt. Beth's uncle worked private security, which meant he spent more time on his feet than strictly healthy babysitting conventions and parties at private venues and even movie theaters. He wasn't licensed to carry a gun, so he didn't have to work any truly dangerous places. He just had to be a presence to keep people in line.

It didn't look like this security guard was licensed to carry a gun either. The train company probably required that the con promoter hire a couple of security guards before they rented the train out for the Unwalker Experience.

"Oh, god," the staffer said as Wolfer put a cold pack he'd found in the room's first aid kit against the bump on the guard's head. "You don't think they threw another zombie off the train, do you?"

"Shouldn't an alarm go off when a window's broken?" I asked.

The picture windows did say they were emergency exits, and most emergency exits had alarms to let other people know that maybe, just maybe, they should make an emergency exit too.

"I don't know," the staffer said. "We didn't get briefed on that."

She looked about ready to jump out of her skin, like Goon One or Goon Two were hiding in the walls ready to attack us at any minute.

"I mean, they could have given us like a what... five-minute overview or something? Here's what you need to know about a train?" She rubbed her hand against her hip. Nothing there except for the waistband of her black pants.

"They didn't even give us walkies because they said we wouldn't need them."

"Doesn't the security guard have a mic?" I asked.

The guard groaned and raised a hand to his head. "The security guard does have a mic," he said without opening his eyes. "Is that bastard still here?"

He started to sit up, but Wolfer put a hand on his shoulder. "Give it a minute," he said.

"What bastard?" the staffer asked.

"The bastard that clocked me," the guard said. "Worst looking zombie on this damn train. Makeup slapped on, didn't even cover up that red face of his."

"Amateur," Wolfer muttered. He'd schooled me on putting on my zombie makeup until I could do it in my sleep.

"Costume all busted out at the seams," the guard said. "Like he was supposed to be some superhero zombie or something."

My shirt was too small for him. I should have realized that and been looking for one of the Marvel zombies, not a *Walking Dead* zombie.

"He didn't throw someone out the window, did he?" the staffer asked.

"Clothes," the guard said. "I caught him throwing clothes out this window! I was doing my rounds, walking through my section, and I caught him going into this room. I knew it was vacant—this last car's only half full—and I knew he wasn't supposed to be back here. Thought maybe he brought a girl back here, then I heard him breaking the glass."

The guard sat up slowly and Wolfer let him, watching the

guy's eyes. I guess to make sure they didn't roll to the back of his head.

"That was it," the guard said. "He knocked me out over some damn clothes."

The clothes he'd worn in my room, that had to be it. He must have realized he'd left evidence behind in our room. Roomette. Whatever.

The guard fingered his earpiece, making sure it was in place, and then triggered his mic. "Rollie?" he said. "You there, man? We got a problem."

He listened for a minute, then repeated the call.

Nothing.

"He's not responding," the guard said to the staffer. "I don't suppose you can reach your people?"

She took a cell phone out of her pocket and stared at it. "No bars," she said. "And no walkie."

Two goons on a train, one in bad zombie cosplay and one dressed as who knew what. Only three staffers, two guards— one currently out of commission and the other one offline— and five hundred partying cosplayers.

I shared a look with Wolfer.

"Houston," I said. "We have one big damn problem."

———

S ometimes being a fan of a zombie show is a good thing.
Besides witnessing some really gnarly deaths, it teaches you how to use found objects as weapons.

Like the squeeze bottle of rubbing alcohol in the first-aid kit.

A shot of rubbing alcohol to the face wouldn't do much to a real zombie, but I was willing to bet it might at least slow down Goon One and his buddy.

Each room had a small first-aid kit, and each kit had a squeeze bottle of rubbing alcohol. We liberated bottles from the all the vacant rooms in the last car, and then the three of us—Wolfer, the staffer, and me—decided to head toward the front of the train.

The security guard, whose name was Horace, wanted to go with us. Wolfer convinced him to stay behind. "You might have a concussion, man," he said. "Better to take care of those old bones, you know?"

"Old bones, my ass," Horace said, but he settled back on the bench seat in another vacant room—one without a busted window—with a groan.

"Just keep trying to reach the guy up front," I said. I really hoped the security guard up front was in better shape than Horace. Or at least was a decade or two younger than Horace and knew a few martial arts.

The private rooms we passed were roomettes like the one Wolfer and I had, and most didn't have the drapes closed on the window in the door, so it was easy to tell which rooms were vacant. The staffer knocked on the few doors with closed drapes, which garnered annoyed looks from the occupants but no goons, either one or two.

That left the party cars—the passenger cars that had turned into party central.

From the look of the snow-covered landscape outside the train and the slight tilt of the floor, we must have just about reached the summit. Truckee was on the other side of the summit but the train wasn't scheduled to stop there. If we could notify the authorities, they might be able to have the train make an emergency stop, although I wasn't real clear on how that worked.

First, though, we had to make it to the front of the train.

Through the party.

We were actually doing pretty good until the Michonne cosplayer I'd seen earlier wrapped her arms around my neck and gave me a boozy smooch on the lips. About the same time a Rick Grimes cosplayer, complete with sheriff's hat and fake radio on his shoulder, spilled a drink that wasn't just soda on the staffer's yellow vest.

"Oh, gawd, I'm so sorry!" he said in a credible Southern accent.

The Michonne cosplayer leaned back and wiped my zombie makeup off her lips. "I got zombie on me!" she cried, laughing at me.

"Zombie cooties!" the crowd around us cried, laughing up a storm.

Wolfer leaned in close to my ear. "I won't tell Beth a thing," he said.

I was about to tell him I sure as hell hoped not since he talked me into this trip in the first place, and that's when I spotted the red face and crappy zombie makeup of Goon One.

He was half a car away, standing in the aisle and pretending to dance with a cosplayer dressed as Carol, complete with short gray wig and a sign that read "Eat my cookies"—a pretty good *Walking Dead* in-joke since Carol on the show looks like a sweet, harmless, grandmotherly type but bakes a mean poisoned cookie when she wants to. (Helpful hint: Not all the villains on *The Walking Dead* are zombies.)

I spotted Goon One about half a second before he spotted me. His eyebrows shot up his forehead—I guess he really thought he'd killed me when he threw this particular zombie from the train—and then he grabbed cosplay Carol around the neck and backed her up against him.

I didn't think the gun he held pressed to her throat was fake.

There were at least a half dozen cosplayers between me and Goon One, and I had no idea where Goon Two was, but I had to do something. The only weapon I had was the squeeze bottle of rubbing alcohol. Even if the bottle could squirt that far, I'd probably hit Carol in the face before I hit Goon One.

Then inspiration struck.

I pointed a finger directly at Goon One and shouted at the top of my lungs. "Whisperer!!"

Whisperers were the absolute worst villains on *The Walking Dead,* in my opinion. Even worse than the cannibals who tried to eat the show's heroes. Whisperers pretended to *be* zombies, going so far as to skin the faces off the zombies and wear them as masks—I know, really gross, right?—when all the while they herded vast numbers of zombies to use as shambling weapons. They cut off the heads of their enemies and left them on stakes to mark their territory.

Whisperers were deadlier than zombies because they were fakes. Just like Goon One.

The partiers in the car went absolutely still for a beat, and then they attacked Goon One.

He didn't stand a chance.

Before he could get a shot off, hands grabbed him from behind and yanked him away from cosplay Carol. She turned around and hit him over the head with a silver serving tray that held a few glued-on fake cookies. Eat my cookies, indeed.

Even Michonne, the same Michonne who'd kissed me, got in on the action. The katana strapped on her back might have been fake, but the straps holding it in place were real leather. She got a strap around one of Goon One's wrists and yanked him face first into the back of a seat. I imagined I heard his skull ring as it hit the metal rung, and then more cosplayers pulled him down on the seat, going in for the kill.

Or at least they would have, if they'd been real zombies.

Right about that time I saw the other security guard barreling down the aisle. I guessed that Horace was finally able to get through on his radio.

This guard was in his thirties and looked like he spent every off hour pumping iron. Muscles upon muscles bulged in his shoulders beneath his black shirt, and his forearms were the size of my thighs. I couldn't even tell if he had a neck.

It didn't take long for Guard Two to break up the melee. He used the straps from Michonne's costume to tie Goon One's arms behind his back. Cosplay Rick Grimes retrieved Goon One's gun from where it had been knocked away and handed it to the security guard, who stuffed it beneath his belt at the small of his back.

One down, one to go?

I managed to work my way to Mr. Muscles, aka Guard Two, to tell him about the second goon, but he was way ahead of me.

"He's under wraps," the guard said. "Caught him trying to get to the conductor." He smiled, a truly terrifying grin since he was a head taller than I was and the grin gave his dark eyes a demented twinkle. "He won't be going anywhere for a while."

Neither, as it turned out, would we.

The train made an emergency stop in Truckee. Goons One and Two were escorted off the train by law enforcement officers, and Wolfer and I gave our statements to another officer who actually managed to take both our costumes and the party that was still going on in most of the train in stride. The con staffer and her two cohorts decided, with the blessing of the law enforcement officers, to let the con-goers off the train to stretch their legs while law enforcement dusted our room—room*ette*—for fingerprints.

Five hundred *Walking Dead* cosplayers. Truckee's a lot smaller than Reno. The town never knew what hit it.

Wolfer stayed on the train even after he'd given his statement. He and the con staffer seemed to be hitting it off, which made me feel good for him. I left them alone while I called my girlfriend. My cell actually had bars, but I kept the call brief. She was in a dressing room in Macy's, trying on an outfit that was actually on clearance, which meant she could afford it.

The day was turning out to be pretty good after all. If, you know, you discounted the fact that I did a Tom Cruise off the side of the train and thought I was going to die.

I have to admit that the rest of the trip was a blast. We

didn't have a lot of free time in Reno because of the stop in Truckee, but the stars—two minor characters that I didn't even remember being in the show—and the director made the commentary lots of fun. I even got to use a private room to catch a few hours sleep on the trip back to Sac. Not our room, since it was still a crime scene, but one of the roomettes in the last car.

Wolfer sat up all night talking with the staffer. They've been going out for six months now, and he's a pretty happy camper.

As for what Goon One and Goon Two were after?

None of the details ever came out in the news or in any story online, but Wolfer found out because the staffer, whose name is Gwen, found out through the grapevine.

"A lottery ticket," she said. "Not for the big one, but nothing to sneeze at."

Goons One and Two, who were roommates, had gone in on a lottery ticket, only to have it stolen. The thief, call him Idiot Zombie Boy, had done it as a prank—Goons One and Two were real jerks to some people in their building who happened to be friends with Idiot Zombie Boy, who figured he'd teach them a lesson.

Fast forward to the day before the Unwalker Experience, and the lottery numbers actually came in. Goons One and Two always played the same numbers, so they knew they'd won some serious money. Now it wasn't just a matter of pride that someone had stolen the ticket from them. There were big bucks on the line.

So they asked around to see if anyone knew anything. Of course, Idiot Zombie Boy's friends caved in the face of Goon

One's anger, and they gave Idiot Zombie Boy away. They even told Goons One and Two where Idiot Zombie Boy would be the following morning—boarding a fandom party train to Reno.

Only Goons One and Two didn't know what Idiot Zombie Boy looked like, just that he was cosplaying as Zombie Merle.

My cosplay. Of course.

Armed only with a Google image of Zombie Merle, Goons One and Two finagled (threatened) a couple of fanboys into selling the goons their boarding passes. Once on the train, Goons One and Two started searching the private rooms of all the Zombie Merle cosplayers. There apparently were a bunch. I just happened to have the rotten luck of interrupting them while they were searching mine.

"Whatever happened to the ticket?" I asked Gwen one night over sushi.

It turned out that Gwen and Beth got along just fine, which worked out for Wolfer and me. We double-dated a couple of times a month, usually going out to eat and then to a movie.

Gwen shrugged. "I'm guessing the guy who stole it cashed it in. It wasn't big enough to make the news, and the guys who attacked you are still in jail."

And would be for a while. Without their lottery winnings, they couldn't make bail.

Couldn't happen to a nicer pair of goons.

Beth turned toward me and arched an eyebrow. "Were you ever going to tell me about Michonne?" she asked. "I hear there was some serious lip-locking going on."

I shot Wolfer a look, then I caught the expression on Gwen's face.

"You..."

I bit down on what I was going to say. She might have given me up, but she was Wolfer's girlfriend, and you don't diss your buddy's girl. Even if she wants to stir up trouble.

I was about to apologize to Beth and beg her forgiveness when I saw the corners of her mouth quirk up in a grin. "Gotcha," she said.

I pulled her toward me for a quick kiss. "Nothing can beat the real thing," I said, and I kissed her again. A little more thoroughly this time just so she'd know I meant it.

Wolfer cleared his throat. "Before you two need a room, what movie are we going to? Did we ever decide?"

Beth and Gwen shared a look. I knew that look. They'd cooked up something.

"There's a new Tom Cruise movie opened last week," Gwen said. "I hear it's pretty good."

"I hear he hangs off a train," Beth said, her expression the picture of total innocence. "Maybe we could go see that so you can tell me what the movie got wrong?"

The girls held their straight looks for half a beat before they dissolved into giggles. Wolfer held out his hands in a don't-blame-me gesture.

Okay, fine. I can live with being compared to a movie star who did all his own crazy stunts for the rest of my life. He might be a god, but I did mine without the benefit of a harness or a wire or anything holding me to the train except my bare hands.

Take that, Mr. Cruise.
Wherever you are.

O'NEIL DE NOUX

O'Neil De Noux takes his amazing skills as one of the best writers of detective fiction working today and gives us another story in the colorful and clearly unique world of Louisiana. The places and events and characters just come alive in O'Neil's fun and powerful stories.

O'Neil has published about fifty novels with more coming regularly. His awards include The United Kingdom Short Story Prize, the Shamus Award (for best private eye fiction), the Derringer Award (for excellence in mystery short fiction) and Police Book of the Year.

Two of his stories have appeared in the prestigious Best American Mystery Stories annual anthology and I noticed he had another in the recommended reading for this last year's volume. He won the Shamus for a story in 2020. You can find out a lot more about his work at his website oneildenoux.com.

THE BONNIE AND CLYDE CAPER

O'NEIL DE NOUX

"So, I hear you're a homicide detective," said the skinny deputy as he stepped up to my booth. "We don't get many killins 'round here."

I put my coffee down. The deputy pulled up his gunbelt and smiled a crooked-tooth grin. His name plate read: Scaddle, and he looked all of twenty-one, minimum age for a commissioned officer in Louisiana.

"Join me." I nodded to the bench-seat across the booth. We were in Parker's Goodtime Café in sunny Arcadia, along US 80 not far from Shreveport, in a part of Louisiana with hills. Parker's was a forties-style diner, looking like an oversized silver torpedo with a row of booths along the windows and a counter and grill on the other side of the center aisle.

The khaki-clad deputy, with a green and yellow Bienville Parish Sheriff's Office patch on his shoulder, sat and extended his right hand. "Glenn Scaddle. Two *Ns* in Glenn and two *Ds* in Scaddle." He was rail-thin with reddish hair and deep-set brown eyes.

"John Raven Beau." We shook hands and I went back to my coffee.

"You really from New Orleans? You sound Cajun with that accent."

"My father was Cajun." I narrowed my light brown eyes. "You seem to know a lot about me, Mr. Scaddle."

He laughed like a donkey and waved to the lone waitress. "Some of that home brew, Peggy." Then turned back to me. "My daddy's Mr. Scaddle. I'm just plain Glenn. Myrtle at the hotel said a big city cop's in town, good-lookin' she said, Mexican lookin'." He glanced around the café. "You fit the script." He seemed proud to have found me in a café with two other customers. "Your mother Mexican? No offense. Spanish are pretty people."

"She's Sioux." I was thinking this deputy was a freaking squirrel.

"Indian?"

"You know any other kind of Sioux?"

Again, the donkey laugh as Peggy the waitress brought his coffee. He took cream and three sugars. I folded my copy of *The Shreveport Times*, figuring Plain Glenn had more to say. Instead, he looked out the window for almost a minute before letting out a low whistle. I turned just as Gillie crossed the narrow street. The blue dress, which she'd lain out before jumping into the shower of our hotel room, was form-fitting. Not a minidress, but short enough to show off those long, sleek legs. Her high heels, and tiny purse hanging from her left shoulder matched her dress color perfectly. With her yellow-blonde hair flowing in long waves as she strolled, lips painted dark red, eyes hidden behind wrap-around sunglasses, she looked as out of place in this small Louisiana town as Marisa Tomei in *My Cousin Vinny*.

"Holy moly," Plain Glenn mumbled, "you gotta love tourist season." He craned his neck to watch Gillie pass and asked, "So, what brings you to our little burg?"

"She did." I nodded toward Gillie as she stepped into the café and came over to slide into the booth next to me. She pulled off her sunglasses and gave me a peck on the lips.

"Sorry I kept you waiting," she said with hint of mischief in those blue eyes. She always kept me waiting but the result was worth the wait.

"Gillian Rahmako. Meet Plain Glenn." We both looked at the deputy who sat with his mouth half-opened in a silly grin. Gillie extended her hand for him to shake, then leaned back as Peggy stepped up. Gillie ordered coffee.

"Don't tell him," Gillie cautioned a confused Plain Glenn as she wrapped her arm around mine and asked, "You won't guess what's going on here this weekend."

"You got me."

"Go ahead and guess." She elbowed me gently.

"All right. Cat rodeo? Shakespeare Festival?"

She poked my side.

"What? Louisiana's lousy with festivals."

Plain Glenn was trying to hide his honk-laugh as Peggy arrived with Gillie's coffee and freshened mine.

Gillie announced, "It's the Authentic Bonnie and Clyde Festival. They were shot just down the road."

I remembered they'd been killed in Louisiana, but I

thought closer to Texas. Gillie looked as proud as Plain Glenn had when he'd found me.

"Is there an <u>Unauthentic</u> Bonnie and Clyde Festival?" I asked.

She playfully poked me again. "I'll bet Mr. Glenn here wouldn't mind escorting me around."

Plain Glenn spit up his coffee, toward the window thankfully. I passed him my napkin and he wiped his face as Gillie apologized and took a sip of her coffee, which was pretty good in Parker's Goodtime Café.

"I thought y'all came for the fest," Plain Glenn said nervously. "That's why so many people are in town."

So many people? Arcadia had a main street, about a dozen blocks long and some side streets, but most of the places were boarded up. I'd seen few people.

"We came for the largest flea market in Louisiana." Gillie pulled a tourist map from her purse. That was Miss Gillian Ann Rahmako's passion, more than any passion I'd been able raise in her. A law degree, in line for a junior partnership at a prestigious maritime law firm, owner of a two-story house just off St. Charles Avenue and a new BMW roadster, Gillie was happiest when browsing flea markets and antique stores, going absolutely giddy over anything ancient, or old at least.

We'd exhausted the flea markets and antique shops in and around New Orleans in the six months we'd been dating. She was thrilled when I took two weeks off to travel with her to Louisiana's largest flea market in Arcadia, Louisiana. I didn't have the heart to tell her I thought she was talking about *Acadiana*, where I'd been raised. Cajun country. But it was nice, on the road with her, talking, snug-

gling in hotel rooms, leaving the sudden violence of home –
back home.

"You can follow the Bonnie and Clyde Trail," Plain Glenn
was saying. "Got twenty points of interest." He nodded down
the street. "They brought the bodies to Conger's Furniture
Store. Had the autopsies there."

"In a furniture store?" I had to ask.

"It sold caskets. Doubled as a funeral home."

Made sense, I guessed.

"Parker's Goodtime Café." Gillie looked around. "Named
for Bonnie Parker?"

"No. Judge Alcee Parker," said Plain Glenn. "No relation.
He's the one who passed the law that women could wear
pants in Louisiana?"

"Law?" Gillie and I said simultaneously.

"Yeah."

Gillie gave me a you-gotta-be-kidding look.

"Before my time," Plain Glenn explained, "but before that
law, women couldn't wear pants in Louisiana."

Whatever. What was the point of discussing it with
someone who really believed that?

Peggy asked if we'd like refills and I shook my head. She
turned to Plain Glenn. "Why aren't you out looking for my
car? All I ask you to do is find one stolen car." She left in a
huff.

I dropped a three dollar tip and scooped up the check for
three dollars, which I paid on the way out. I slipped on my
dark Ray Bans and noticed I stood a good eight inches taller
than Plain Glenn. At six-two, I was a good half-foot taller
than Gillie in her high heels.

Gillie slipped her sunglasses back on and asked our deputy, "Where is that furniture store slash funeral parlor?"

Plain Glenn looked a little embarrassed. "It was torn down after a tornado hit it back in '92. Fools shoulda fixed it up. There's a vacant lot there. There's talk of turning it into a park."

Gillie laughed and wrapped her arm around Plain Glenn's right arm and her other around my left arm and said, "Well, let's go see the vacant lot."

"Well, whatever y'all do, y'all gotta see the re-enactment of the shootout at three o'clock." Plain Glenn beamed. "Can't miss the crowd of cars leavin' town. Just follow the traffic."

———

We finally shed ourselves of Plain Glenn as we arrived at the largest outdoor flea market in Louisiana, which ran nine blocks, both sides of First Street, the main drag in Arcadia. I tagged along as Gillie went from table to table, examining lamps, jewelry, and books. By ten a.m., it was really hot, the sky void of clouds. Thankfully a warm breeze blew through town, cooling the sweat on the short-sleeved shirt I wore hanging out over my black tee-shirt to hide my off-duty nine-millimeter tucked into my belt at the small of my back. Gillie didn't sweat. Perspiration was a stranger to beautiful women.

Arcadia played the Bonnie and Clyde card to the max with side streets named Ambush Alley, Desperado Drive and Barrow Boulevard, which was little more than an alley. Most of the storefronts were boarded up. Broken windows, jagged glass hanging from some, like vacant eyes staring blindly at the passing years. The lone filling station was defunct, the price listed for regular gas was ninety-seven cents.

Gillie bought a pair of vintage sunglasses, cat-eye style with blue frames the same color as her dress. She put on the glasses immediately, retiring her wrap-arounds to her purse. I picked up an Elmore Leonard paperback I hadn't read.

OK, north Louisiana wasn't my idea of a vacation spot, but the long drive with Gillie, getting away from New Orleans and the constant pressure-cooker of homicide work relaxed me. But I could never turn off the cop in me. I spotted a pickpocket at the flea market. Unshaven, with oily black hair, a good three inches taller than me, skinnier than Plan Glenn and wearing a blindingly orange sport coat over dirty jeans and ratty running shoes, he tried his best to blend into the crowd. There were dozens of people in town by that time. He blended as easily as giraffe at a dog show.

Gillie did a double-take. "What's with the unnecessarily orange jacket? Kind of warm for wool, wouldn't you say?"

"Exactly."

Orange-man checked out several men at a table of vintage magazines, sidling up to a man in a lime-green shirt and baggy shorts, bumped into him and neatly extracted the man's wallet from a rear pocket. He turned, took two steps and bumped into me. Pretending to swing around him, I grabbed the lapels of his jacket and kicked his feet out from under him, landing on his chest with my knees, my nine-millimeter pressed against his jaw.

His eyes met mine and I smiled coldly. "Don't move."

Standing in front of us, Gillie turned and called out, "Plain

Glenn!" She only had to call once and I heard the jiggling of keys and the slap of the deputy's holster and he raced up. Hadn't realized he wore cowboy boots.

"What happened?" Plain Glenn reached for his revolver, but hesitated, thankfully.

I slid my weapon back into my belt. "Handcuffs."

Plain Glenn fumbled out his cuffs and passed them to me. I rolled orange-man over, cuffed him behind his back and patted him down, coming up with three wallets but no weapons. I pulled the man up and turned him to face me before saying, "You're supposed to keep the money and throw the wallets away, moron." Spotting the man with the lime-green shirt, I held up the wallets. "Which one's yours?"

———————

Painted canary yellow, Cole's Pharmacy was the only bright building in Arcadia. It occupied the entire first floor of a raised Victorian at the corner of Barrow Boulevard and Ford Deluxe Avenue.

"Bet ya' they were shot in a Ford Deluxe," Gillie said as I opened the door for her. One step inside, we stopped immediately. I'm not sure what a turn-of-the-century pharmacy supposed to look like, but we stood there a minute to take it all in. It seemed like a movie set, pristine hardwood floors, white shelving with pharmaceuticals on the right, on the left a marble counter with a soda fountain, manned by a tall gentleman in all white, including his hair and full moustache turned up on the ends. He nodded to us.

There was even a wooden Indian just inside the doorway.

Couldn't be Sioux, wearing a thick, buckskin shirt and long buckskin pants. The face wasn't lean either, like a plains warrior. It was flat, looked exotic, more like a Mexican. Pretty people, right?

Gillie breezed over to the counter, took off her sunglasses and asked the man, "Could I get a cherry phosphate?"

"You sure can." He didn't smile exactly, but the chiseled face softened as Gillie climbed up on a stool.

"Make it two," she said, patting the stool next to her. I took the hint as she asked the man, "You Mr. Cole?"

"Actually, I am. Pharmacist, cashier, soda fountain jerk. I sweep the place too."

I sat and watched him fill two glasses with fizzy water, pour in some red syrup, mix them, then add shaved ice before bringing them to us with two straws. Gillie took a sip and laughed. "Good as where I grew up."

"Where's that?" Cole asked, wiping the marble counter with a white dishtowel.

"Manhattan, Kansas." She took another sip. "So, what's good for lunch here?"

Cole passed us two plastic-coated menus. "Sandwiches and salads only. The BLT is my specialty. Cooked the bacon a short while ago, still warm in the rotisserie."

Gillie ordered the Caesar salad and I ordered Cole's special BLT, both of us sipping our phosphates and watching the elderly man fix our food with an economy of motion. We finished the sweet-tangy drinks at the same time. I'd never tasted a soft drink like it. Back home, Barq's red drink was much sweeter.

I felt Gillie's hand on my arm as she said, "You know what I'm thinking?"

I started chuckling.

"What's so funny?"

"If <u>any</u> man could tell what a woman's thinking, it would be a miracle."

She poked my chest with a bony knuckle. "Your brain's too slow."

I grinned. "I knew it was something like that."

She put and elbow up on the counter, cupped her chin in the palm of her hand and said, "I was thinking about our knee. I checked up on you."

I was right. I never would have figured what she was thinking.

"All-state quarterback in high school. Full scholarship to LSU. *Sports Today* called you the top prospect in the south, rocket arm, the best running-quarterback in a decade. No wonder you moved so fast with that pickpocket, had him down in a heartbeat."

She gave me a serious look. "I found an article about your knee too." Those blue eyes stared into mine. "You never explained the scars on your knee. That why you didn't finish at LSU?"

"That and my slow brain."

She poked me again.

Mr. Cole arrived with our meals and left them with fresh cherry phosphates. He'd fixed the BLT on a toasted roll, crisp bacon, crisper lettuce, chilled tomatoes, light mayonnaise and a touch of mustard. As I took the second bite of the best BLT I'd ever tasted two people rushed into Cole's. A man in a light-weight tan suit and a blonde woman in a pink dress shuffled up to us and introduced themselves as Bill Sutherland, who played Clyde Barrow in the shootout for ten years before moving on to become the festival's manager, and Casey Quail, who used to play Bonnie Parker.

Sutherland was about five-six, with slicked black hair and a pencil-thin moustache. Quail, a pretty woman with green eyes, announced she'd put on too much weight to play Bonnie and was now the festival's public relations coordinator. She wasn't heavy at all, but I learned long ago that most women thought they were too heavy. Both looked about forty.

"Just wanted to shake your hand," Sutherland said. "Catching that pickpocket was boss. Really boss." I held up my BLT in lieu of shaking his hand.

"He could have been spotted from the space shuttle," Gillie said with a twist of her head, flipping her hair aside, "in that jacket."

Sutherland laughed a little too loud. They sat at the counter on either side of us. The woman wore too much perfume, sweet, flowery, like the strong stuff worn by my Cajun aunts. Sutherland continued his congratulating, telling us we showed the tourists crime didn't pay in Arcadia. "That gun you carry, you some kinda cop, right? Federal?"

"NOPD."

"Huh."

I explained and noticed the two women communicating with their eyes past me, exchanging glances that, I'm sure, said a lot, but were completely indecipherable to me. The looks didn't look friendly.

"Y'all can't miss the shootout at three," Sutherland was saying. "It's the highlight of the fest."

I nodded as I finished off my BLT and noticed Gillie had put away a lot of her salad. She was a sneaky eater, little bites, but she got it all down. I, on the other hand, ate like a cop. Fast and furiously because you never knew when you'd get called away from a lunch break to stop a crime or protect the public – from the public.

Mr. Cole brought us the check and Gillie snatched it up because I kept paying for everything. She put down a credit card and Mr. Cole told her no credit cards, no checks. Cash only. I passed him a twenty before she could dig out any bills from her purse and told him that was the best BLT I ever had.

"You don't tip me. I'm the owner."

"I'm not tipping the owner." I stood and backed away from the counter. "I'm tipping the guy who served us."

Quail stepped away with me, as I tried to let Gillie finish her salad in peace but Sutherland stayed with her. She politely listened to his jabbering. Quail accidentally brushed against me, then backed off with a coy blush on her face. Jesus!

"Did you see the wooden Indian?" she asked.

I told her no and she directed me to it, telling me it was one of those Indians from *The Last of the Mohicans*. Not the book, but the movie with Daniel Day Lewis.

"Weren't those Hurons, Ottawa, Mohawks? Mostly bald or with, you know, Mohawks."

"I guess," she shrugged as we arrived at the Indian. Sutherland came over with a disposable camera, asking me to pose with Quail and the Indian. I looked back at Gillie for help but she just waved.

Eventually, we left Cole's, back into the bright sun and thick humidity, Gillie looking back inside. "What a great place."

Sutherland glanced back at the pharmacy. "Cole's a weird duck. Only taking cash."

Quail seemed annoyed at him, glanced at her watch and declared, "We have to be off."

Sutherland shook my hand and said, "Our deputy can lead you to the shootout, show you the way."

Quail batted her eyes and gave my hand a secret squeeze before leaving with Sutherland.

Gillie and I headed back to the flea market and ran right into Plain Glenn. "Y'all come from Cole's?"

Gillie told him she thought it was such a cool place.

"The old skin-flint only takes cash," said Plain Glenn. "Keeps it all in a big safe in back. Bought it from the bank when it went belly up. Had to tear the back of his place down and rebuild it around the safe. Y'all can ride with me to the shootout. It'll be crowded by the monument."

Gillie said, "That's all right. I'll drive." We started walking again and she asked, "What model of car were Bonnie and Clyde killed in?"

The crooked-tooth grin was back. "A 1934 Ford Deluxe, V-8. You should see it. A hundred a sixty bullets in it."

"Ford Deluxe." Gillie gave me a knowing smirk. "Is the car here in Arcadia?"

Plain Glenn let out a long breath. "No. Las Vegas. But I saw it once."

W e passed the Bonnie & Clyde RV Trailer Park with its huge sign, a silhouette of the bandit-couple, holes in their torsos. The park looked crowded. Gillie tooled her roadster down LA 154, a narrow black-top, two-lane road which probably hadn't change much since that fateful day back in 1934. We hit the traffic just outside Gibsland, which was closer to the site of the shooting, both burgs nestled between longs stretches of piney woods. The site of the shooting was about seven miles south of Gibsland, the last town Bonnie and Clyde visited, according to the brochures we picked up at the flea market.

Bienville Parish sheriff's deputies, including a dark-haired sergeant and Plain Glenn, directed traffic as cars parked on either side of the road. The sergeant flagged us down and told us to go back and park alongside the road heading back toward Gibsland because they had to clear an area by the monument for the re-enactment.

Gillie u-turned and we parked and walked back. It was then I saw a line of rain clouds in the west, dark gray and menacing and heading our way. By the time we eased through the crowd at the monument, I could smell the rain, stronger than the scent of pine. Families were taking turns posing next to the monument, a chipped granite marker, some of the lettering hard to read.

"Are those bullet holes?" Gillie asked, pulling my hand as we crossed the road.

"Probably. Perfect target."

"This site," Gillie read aloud from the engraving, "May 23, 1934. Clyde Barrow And Bonnie Parker Were Killed By Law

Enforcement Officials. Erected by Bienville Parish Police Jury."

I spotted Myrtle, the one who knew all about me from the hotel, standing with Mr. Cole. She nodded but he didn't seem to notice us. Several of the vendors from the flea market were there too and a lot of kids. Hell, this was clean American fun. A shootout.

A voice over a bull horn blared, "All right, everyone." It was Plain Glenn. "Everyone has to retreat beyond where the police cars are parked for the re-enactment."

We followed the crowd back across the road and eased toward our car as the sky darkened. Lightning flashed in the distance, followed a few seconds later by a roll of thunder. The crowd looked big now.

"Where's our festival manager and his plump public relations coordinator?" Gillie said.

"She's not that plump." I looked around but couldn't spot Sutherland or Quail.

"Without that girdle, I'll bet she has quite a belly."

The bullhorn crackled again. "Here they come!"

We all looked down the road as a black car approached slowly. Looked more like a Model-T to me than a Ford Deluxe, not that I knew what a Deluxe looked like, expect it was probably bigger. A movement to my left caught my eye as six men carrying rifles and Thompson sub-machine guns with round carriages protruding from the bottom, like gangsters from a Cagney movie, came out of the woods and leveled their guns at the approaching car.

Gillie said, "Didn't even ask them to surrender."

The first gun went off, its loud report causing everyone to

flinch. The car swerved, the lawmen opened up, fusillade so loud I felt it in my teeth. As the gunfire slackened, I heard a couple kids crying from the loud noise and noticed holes in the car.

"I didn't see any of those little explosions in the car, like in the movie," Gillie said.

The car's windows were shattered, the holes probably there all along. The air reeked of cordite and burned gunpowder. As the car came to a creeping stop, just this side of the monument, the passenger door fell open and we saw the red-headed faux-Bonnie slumped in the seat. Clyde jumped out of the car and swung his own tommy-gun toward the lawmen, who opened up again. He shimmied and dropped the gun and fell on his back.

Two of the lawmen closed in, firing at both corpses until they were out of ammo. The actors convulsed as if struck by bullets. As the coppers checked the bodies, a fat drop of rain fell in the roadway a few feet from us. Gillie immediately dug her keys out of her purse and we headed for the car. We just got in when the rain hit, like God had turned on a fire hose, washing across the window in a waves. Thunder slammed outside and forked lightning danced above as Gillie eased on to the black top and tooled us right out of there. We left the storm by the time we reached Gibsland, but the sky behind us was charcoal gray.

"Tornado weather," Gillie said, a catch in her voice. She would know, being from Kansas.

"Ever see one?"

"Up close and personal." She told me how a big twister had caught her family on the open road, how her father pulled

The Bonnie and Clyde Caper

their pick-up under a train trestle and how they went to hide under the trestle as the twister skipped by.

"It didn't come any closer than a football field, but it nearly yanked me and my little sister away." She looked pale, then shrugged. "Didn't mean to get all maudlin."

I reached around to rub her neck gently. "Maudlin? Why not? You just saw the most famous couple around here get slaughtered."

She giggled nervously. A few minutes later, I looked back and saw the sky wasn't as dark behind us as we pulled into Arcadia. The storm was headed north. Gillie braked hard, turning me around. In the center of the road stood Peggy in her aqua waitress outfit. Face red, panting as if she'd run a mile, she came to my side of the car as I rolled the window down.

"Where's ... Deputy ... Scaddle?" She wheezed.

"What's wrong?"

"My stolen ... car." She sucked in a deep breath and pointed up the street. "Parked ... behind Cole's."

"We'll check it out." I'd let her in if we weren't in a two-seater.

She nodded and backed away, pointing in the direction of Barrow Boulevard. We were there in a minute, Gillie turned on Ford Deluxe, pulling into the shell parking lot behind Cole's where we saw a baby-blue Ford Taurus with a red fender. I got out before Gillie turned off the engine, and for the second time that day, drew my weapon. A screwdriver protruded from the shattered starter housing. I smelled something, took another whiff. Perfume. A strong, familiar scent. Then I smelled smoke.

"It's coming from Cole's!" Gillie pointed to smoke slithering from the back door of the pharmacy.

As we started for the door, it slammed open and two figures in yellow plastic suits stumbled out on the back porch. Wearing hoods with face-plates and gloves, they looked like spacemen from a bad science fiction movie. I raised my weapon as one yanked off its hood and slapped the other with the hood. Quail wailed at the other figure, "Idiot! You set the money on fire."

Sutherland pulled his mask off and staggered across the porch. He gasped, "Damn thing doesn't work!"

"It's not a gas mask, you nincompoop," Quail yelled and then saw us and froze. She pointed at Sutherland. "He set the money on fire."

"Down," I told them. "On your stomachs." Aiming my weapon at each, back and forth until they complied. Gillie tip-toed past both and peeked into Cole's. Then she went in.

I moved between my two prisoners and shouted to Gillie, "Is it bad in there?"

"No! Just inside the safe."

I told Quail and Sutherland to stop wiggling. Sutherland coughed again. I heard two coughs inside and then a loud clang.

"You all right?"

Gillie bounced into the doorway and smiled. "Yeah. I shut the safe. No oxygen, the fire should go out." She folded her arms and looked at our prisoners. "There's an acetylene torch on the floor. It opened the safe all right."

"How?" Sutherland coughed again. "How'd you know?"

"The smoke, you moron!" Quail sat up and tried to kick him, only he was too far away. "He burned the money!"

"Lie back down," I growled, then leaned over and searched Sutherland. I asked Gillie to frisk Quail.

"Like hell she will." Quail sat up again.

"Either she does or I do," I said and immediately knew that was a mistake.

"You can." There was a flirtatious lilt to her angry voice.

I nodded to Gillie who put a foot on Quail's back, shoved her down and then frisked her. Rushing footsteps turned me in time to see Plain Glenn and the Bienville sergeant lope into the rear parking area of Cole's, both with guns out. I put mine away immediately. Before I could say a word, Peggy and Myrtle from the hotel, Lord knows where she came from, intercepted the rushing cops.

For the next two minutes, I timed them, Peggy and Myrtle lit into Plain Glenn and the sergeant about the stolen car, about rampant crime in Arcadia, about Plain Glenn not even knowing how to tip a waitress, about the upcoming election and how they planned to vote the sheriff out of office if these were the best he could come up with as deputies.

"Why steal my car?" Peggy moaned. "They ruined the steering column."

It was Gillie who ran out of patience first. "They stole it as a getaway car. Drive to where they stashed their car."

Peggy and Myrtle looked at us as the cops took the opportunity to join us on the porch.

"What's that smoke?" asked the sergeant, who's name tag read – LeBeau. Gillie told him these two broke in and set a fire inside, but it's out now. I helped Plain Glenn handcuff the two desperados and stand them up.

A maroon car that looked like a vintage Rolls Royce came into the parking area. Cole was behind the wheel and I saw it wasn't a Rolls at all. A heart-shaped grille, the car had flared fenders and split front bumpers.

Cole climbed out and stood there a few seconds. I started to tell him about the break-in when Plain Glenn interrupted, "Looks like they went in that back window. Put an acetylene torch to your bank safe. They went out of their way to suggest Officer Beau here, he's a New Orleans detective, go to the re-enactment so none of us cops would be around. Even stole a car as a getaway." He pointed to Peggy's Taurus. "Screwdriver to the steering column."

I glanced at Gillie who was looking around for the window. We spotted it at the far end of the building away from all the action. Plain Glenn's vision was very good, even when he wasn't checking out my girlfriend.

Cole stepped up on the porch and growled, "It's not a bank safe. Just a walk-in safe. No time lock."

"I'm afraid all the contents of your safe got burned," Gillie told Cole. He turned to the two in the yellow jumpsuits with a cold glare.

"You see what was inside before you torched it?" he asked.

Sutherland looked away. Quail said no.

"Only money in there was yesterday's receipts and that's insured," Cole said, looking at Plain Glenn now. "I'm not idiotic enough to keep all my money in a safe in my store. That why we got banks in Shreveport."

The good deputy couldn't mask his surprise as he pulled

up his gunbelt and said that was good, smart, the way to go. He turned to me and I said it was boss. "Really boss."

Cole went inside to check it out as LeBeau took Sutherland by the arm, letting Plain Glenn take Quail's elbow as they led them away. Gillie started toward the window used to enter Cole's and I followed. The screen was on the ground, the window jimmied from the outside.

"How do you suppose they knew Cole didn't have an alarm?" Gillie narrowed those blue eyes at me. I took a closer look at the window. There were no alarm strips but that meant nothing these days with motion detectors and alarms triggered by sound.

"Come on," I said, taking her hand.

"Where are we going?"

"Police station."

We headed for her car. Gillie asked, "What's does, 'It's boss. Really boss,' mean?"

"You got me. But look who's been saying it."

It wasn't much of a police station, a single-story, cinderblock building along Ambush Alley just off First Street. Crammed inside the office were LeBeau, Plain Glenn, Myrtle, Peggy and three men I recognized as operators of the flea market. I could see into the two cells and they were empty.

"What happened to tweedle-dumb and tweedle-dumber?" Gillie asked as the men made way for us.

LeBeau waved to two doors behind him. "Locked in the interview rooms. We're letting them simmer."

I eased over to LeBeau and said, "I think we should talk with Quail first."

"Who?" He smelled of Old Spice and faintly of cigar smoke.

"The woman."

He nodded. "What's your name again?"

I pulled out my credentials.

"Beau? Cajun, huh?"

"Born and raised on Vermilion Bay."

He stuck out his hand. "I'm from St. Martinville." Evangeline country. Couldn't get more Cajun than that. He eased toward the first interview room and said, "Let's talk to the woman."

Casey Quail was climbing out of her yellow spacesuit as we came in. She wore a tee-shirt and shorts underneath, both gray, both sweat-stained. The small room reeked of her perfume and perspiration. No girdle and she's wasn't plump. Solid, but not plump and no big belly. Had to remember to tell Gillie that. LeBeau took the only chair and let Quail stand, her back against the wall, me standing against the door.

Red-faced, she looked at me, then LeBeau as he casually took out his ID folder, withdrew a Miranda card and read her rights aloud. She watched me and I stared back, unemotional and dead-serious. She tried a quivering smile, then exhaled deeply. She rolled her shoulders and her breasts. LeBeau finished and looked at me. I kept my expressionless, unblinking stare on Quail for a full minute. She let out another sigh.

"So?" she said. "It was a practical joke."

"Try again." The look I gave her came naturally. A plains warrior never revealed emotion in battle, except to war whoop, which wasn't called for here. No way I could just throw back my head and go, "Hi-yaa! Hi-yaa!" No, this called for the stone-serious stare.

"It was Sutherland's fault. All of it." She folded her arms in a defensive position.

"Yeah?" I said.

"He talked me into it. He can be very persuasive."

Since she gave me an opening, I took it. "As persuasive as he'll probably be with the D.A., putting it all on you. You know the story, Eve tempting Adam with the apple in the Garden of Eden." Jesus, I couldn't believe I said that. But it worked.

She teared-up and I knew we were almost there. I leaned closer and let a sympathetic smile crawl across my lips before saying, "It wasn't all Sutherland's idea, was it?"

She wiped the tears from her eyes and went, "Huh?"

"It wasn't yours either. It was Scaddle, wasn't it?"

She looked at LeBeau who looked as surprised as she, then turned back at me and I told her, "I'm a detective, Casey. That's why Scaddle sought me out, was so determined for me to see the re-enactment. He mentioned it before Sutherland. Last thing he wanted was someone like me in town."

She leaned back against the wall, hands by her sides now and said, "How'd you know?"

LeBeau produced a mine-cassette recorder and we took her statement. Then we stepped out to put Casey Quail into one of the cells and found Mr. Cole explaining to Gillie that his car was a Brewster, 1936 model, built on a Rolls Royce chassis. Rolls owned Brewster. Deputy Plain Glenn Scaddle was leaning against the only desk in the place.

"Ramko," Plain Glenn interrupted Cole, "What kinda name is that?"

"Rahmako," Gillie corrected him. "It's Finnish."

"Huh?" Plain Glenn noticed me and LeBeau and leaned away from my girlfriend.

"From Finland."

"Oh," he said and I could see he had no clue. Louisiana schools weren't strong on geography."

"I'm a Scot," Plain Glenn said, tugging up his gunbelt. "From Scotland. Long time ago."

I moved to pass him, unsnapped his holster and palmed his weapon before he could react. I handed it, butt first, to LeBeau. Plain Glenn slapped his holster a moment too late.

"You're wanna pull a gun on me?" Over my shoulder, I told LeBeau, "Give it back to him." My hand eased around to my weapon. Plain Glenn raised both hands and tried to chuckle.

"Whoa, cowboy. What's goin' on?"

I put a hand on his shoulder and stared into his eyes. "We're going into that little room and you're going to tell Sergeant LeBeau and me all about it." I squeezed his shoulder until he winced. "Don't insult our intelligence with a cock-and-bull story. And never call me a cowboy again. I'm Sioux."

LeBeau took him into the room. Gillie grabbed my hand as I started to follow. "Plain Glenn isn't so plain, is he?"

"Nope," I told her.

"He knows too much, bragging how it all went down, how the window was jimmied. Peggy's car, the broken steering column and he never went near the car." She pointed her chin at me. "How could he see the window jimmied from the porch?"

"How'd he know they used an acetylene torch?"

I brush-kissed her lips and told her I'd be a few minutes.

Deputy Scaddle, looking much younger than twenty-one, more like an errant teen-ager, confessed almost immediately. All it took was me saying he was pretty smart about it all, nearly pulled off the caper of the century in Arcadia. How was he to know Cole didn't keep his money in there and that Sutherland didn't know squat about using an acetylene? I didn't mention how would he know someone like me would be in town.

"Clyde Barrow would have been proud of you," I added. "You almost made it."

Again the crooked-tooth grin, the fool appeared pleased with himself. LeBeau took his confession before booking all three. Gillie was wired, bouncing as we walked out of the jail.

"You all right?"

"I will be, soon as we get to the room."

I almost asked what she meant, but caught myself. It was there in her eyes. The firelight of lust hovered in those baby blues. She squeezed my hand and walked faster, towing me toward the hotel. It was definitely time to turn on my French side.

After, as we lay in bed, the ceiling fan cooling us, Gillie wouldn't stop talking. Not about us or about Bonnie and Clyde or even the caper. She kept talking about the maroon Brewster and Cole's marble counter and soda fountain and the old man's handle-bar moustache. She sure liked old things.

For a moment, I wondered if I'd be catching a bus back to New Orleans.

ROB VAGLE

Rob Vagle is a veteran short story writer who is becoming a regular contributor to these pages, something I am very happy about. I feel lucky to have his work here. And you will understand that after reading this fantastic story.

His stories are all different and all powerful in a Pulphouse sort of way.

I suggest you go to robvagle.com to find out a lot more about his fantastic stories and books.

CONFESSIONAL

ROB VAGLE

What was wrong with Patrick Sanders?

He found he liked to ask himself this question using the third person, which in turn, made him count the number of strange behaviors he engaged in.

For instance, his routine visit to the first floor men's restroom at Massey hall. There were no classrooms in Massey and it housed academic and administrative departments of the College of Liberal Arts and Sciences. That fact meant the building was quiet with less people around then, say, a building with classrooms in it.

Massey Hall, the beige brick building with architecture from the nineteen fifties on the outside and carpeted hallways and sheetrock walls on the inside. Massey used to house students over sixty years ago. Today, after knocking down walls and erecting new ones and general rearrangement of the interior, a new visitor wouldn't have suspected that.

None of this interested Patrick. The only part of Massey

Hall that interested him was the first floor men's restroom. Because of the quiet.

When Patrick entered the men's room it smelled like bleach, soap, and toilet disinfectant. The scent was so strong it tickled the inside of his nose and he sneezed into this elbow, the sound of him loud and explosive in the cool, damp room. The one inch tiles on the floor, brown and beige, were still damp from a mop.

He assumed the janitors had just cleaned it, but wondered, with the overkill of cleaning supplies, if they had washed away copious amounts of blood and disposed of a body.

The men's room appeared to be empty—nobody standing at the two urinals separated by a panel wall and no feet on the floor in the two toilet stalls.

This was all well and good for Patrick because everything about the first floor men's room in Massey Hall had become routine. It was the place he went this semester between his nine o'clock and eleven o'clock class on the ASU campus.

For Patrick, the men's room at Massey was a literal rest stop between his class at business and his art class at Neeb North. His bowels didn't have to do business often during this hour window of time, but he did enjoy the solitude of checking his messages (text and email) on his phone. In other words: Thumb-fucking his phone, his girlfriend, Kim, called it.

Inside the second stall, Patrick could have used the time to reflect on why he did things he did, but instead he sat on the toilet seat with his pants still on and pulled out his phone to do the deed Kim complained Patrick performed at restaurant tables and in bed.

So much for introspection. Patrick was aware of that thought as he pulled open his inbox to check his email. What will be will be.

However, he then noticed he wasn't alone in the men's room. Somebody was in the other stall. The man wore shiny black loafers and Patrick hadn't heard him come in and he was certain the other bathroom stall had been empty a moment before.

He shook his head and chalked it up to not being aware of his surroundings. Which made sense with Kim's complaining about him thumb-fucking his phone every moment of the day. How could he be aware of everything around him?

"Please absolve me of my sins," the man next door said.

Great, Patrick thought, the dude is talking on his phone.

Then the man said again, "Please. Please forgive me. Are you there?"

The man's voice sounded sad and loud in the men's room which wasn't designed as a confessional. A confessional would be more intimate. Contained. Like a coffin.

Patrick froze, phone in one hand, other hand under his chin. He gave a side eye at the wall next to him with the man behind it. He hoped the dude would shut up.

"Hello. I know you're there," the man said.

"You do know you're in a men's restroom, right? And I'm no frickin' priest," Patrick said.

"I don't need a priest. I just need someone to absolve me of my sins," the man said.

"I'm not that dude," Patrick said.

His solitary moment in the Massey Hall restroom was ruined. He felt it slip away like the drop of a towel. If he had wanted conversation he would have used the rest room in Memorial Union.

"You are," said the man on the other side.

"If anyone will do, go find someone else. Leave me in peace, so I can finish my business," Patrick said.

"Listen to me," the man said.

Light drumming came from the wall, it sounded like the man was drumming his fingertips against it. Patrick didn't know if the wall was made of some heavy duty fiberglass or some composite involving metal. The walls had a gleam, like a metallic surface, and on Patrick's side he could just make out his shadowy reflection in the wall and the graffiti written there. Not products of hight art, but low brow, fitting for late-stage teenagers and young adults who hadn't grown out of their juvenile stage, with drawings of male and female genitalia.

Patrick had enough of this conversation. He reached back and lowered the flush handle (that was a habit of his in that he didn't want anyone else in the restroom to think he was actually just sitting there, or worse, didn't flush) and reached for the stall door.

The chrome slider wouldn't move. He jiggled it, but it felt as if a magnet kept the door sealed shut.

"Listen to my story," the man said next door.

Patrick slipped his phone in his pants pocket and with a deep, fortifying breath of air that still smelled like cleaning supplies, he got down on his hands and knees. The thought of his bare hands on the tiled floor of the rest room disgusted him, but a stuck door would not keep him there.

Once on his hands and knees he realized he also had to

put his forearms on the floor to get under the door. His face twisted in disgust as he mentally added his forearms to the body parts that would need a soapy wash.

The moment he edged his hands out from underneath the stall door, a pair of shoes—Keds written on the sides--walked by, nearly stepping on his fingers. Reflectively, Patrick pulled back and realized the men's room had two new visitors.

"Your pop know about it?" Someone asked. It was a young voice, younger than the older adult one Patrick had heard in the stall next door.

"Hell no. He'd tear my head off and shit down my neck if he did," said another young voice.

"I'm the one with the filthy mouth," the man next door said.

Patrick sound down hard onto the toilet seat. At first he didn't like how the bathroom suddenly grew crowded and he was being forced in a conversation he didn't want to have. He held his breath with a sinking feeling something odd was going on.

For one, the floor seemed cleaner, with more shine. The cleaning smell wasn't as pungent as a moment before. And the two college students outside the stall were talking as if they hadn't heard the dude in the next stall.

"He'll never know," filthy mouth said. "Why do you care? I have the cash now and you said you'd do it. That's the deal, right, asshole?

"Make sure he doesn't find out," the other voice said. "Nothing leads back to me."

Their shadows lay on the one-inch-tile floor and they looked like stick legs of child's drawing. Patrick faked a cough. And coughed again when there was no reaction from the outside. He felt ridiculous doing it. The two outside exchanged something, Patrick saw it by the shadows of their hands as they stood in front of the sinks and mirror.

"When will they be gone?" filthy mouth asked.

"They'll be gone by Sunday morning," said the other.

When the voice of the man next door spoke again, Patrick turned his head to the wall. "That was Wednesday, April nineteenth, nineteen sixty one," the man said. "On Saturday night just after nine o'clock on April twenty second, nineteen sixty one, Billy Martin and Elaine Crenshaw die in a car crash when the brakes fail. Look it up on your phone if you want to have proof."

Patrick looked to the tiled floor again and the shadows were gone and the floor was dingy again, the tiles less vibrant, now faded.

"Are you looking?" asked the man in the next stall.

"Why do I care, man?" Patrick asked.

Someone with bare feet walked by Patrick's stall. The toenails were long and the big toe had long black hairs on it. The person went to the stall next to Patrick's, the one where the man sat, but the shoes were gone at the base of the toilet.

Bare Feet sat on the toilet and Patrick reached for the stall door handle to see if he could get out now. His mind couldn't process what was happening. It all seemed like a dream or a hallucination.

But before he could try the slider, the first floor men's room in Massey Hall exploded with a gun shot. Patrick flinched and dropped his phone. His ears rang, but not before he heard something splatter in the next stall.

Then the air smelled like smoke and iron.

He bent over to pick up his phone and noticed the bare feet in the stall next door. Blood droplets were on the floor and a revolver had landed on the tiles between those two bare feet. One foot, the right one, wasn't flat on the floor, but on its right edge.

The red, scarlet blood screamed at him and he picked up his phone and threw himself into the stall door. The slider still wouldn't work and he pounded, pounded on the door.

"I'm not finished," said the man in the next stall. "Tuesday, May second, nineteen sixty one. The law caught up to Dexter. That was guy I paid to rig the brakes and cause the car crash. I wasn't anywhere to be found. The police were working hard at finding a motive. Dexter couldn't wait it out. He thought his life was over, thought he was going to the electric chair." The man chuckled, then continued, "He wasn't concerned about the loss of life. Just more concerned about his own ruined life."

"None of this concerns me," Patrick said. "I don't need to know this."

The man said, "You have your phone. But who are we kidding. You kids these days have a computer in your pocket. Use your pocket computer and you'll find the information I gave you accurate."

Patrick looked at his phone. The screen lit up with the wallpaper of him and Kim clinging to each other. The screen wasn't cracked thanks to the Otter protective case.

He tried the stall door again. The slider wouldn't move.

"If I look up your information, will you let me go?" Patrick asked.

"In due time."

What did that mean?

Patrick brought up Google on his phone and did a search. And after two flustered attempts with the information he had gotten from the man in the stall next door, he found a link about an unsolved mystery on the ASU campus involving a Dexter Snider and the couple who died in the car crash in nineteen sixty one. After Dexter's suicide, his alibi panned out, but there was evidence he was the one who tampered with the brakes. They also found evidence, Dexter had done other unscrupulous services on other vehicles. But the murder of Billy Martin and Elaine Crenshaw remains unsolved.

"Did you find it?" The man asked.

"You're right," Patrick said. "Everything as you said. The case is unsolved. Can I leave now?"

"Will you absolve me?" The man asked.

Patrick realized he didn't know the man's name. Even if he knew it, the police wouldn't take his word for it. A cold case fifty years old they would want to know how Patrick knew.

"Will you absolve me?" The man asked again.

In an instant the answer came to Patrick's lips. "No. I can't. I won't. It's not my place."

Patrick stopped himself from saying he thought the man in the stall next to him should go to hell.

Then the man said, "Thank you for listening."

The slider on the stall door slipped back on its own and the door squeaked open an inch. Patrick pushed the door further open and saw himself in the mirror above the sink. His face was pale and he looked like he had seen a ghost.

The shoes in the stall next to him were gone.

He never told another soul about what had happened to him in the first floor men's restroom in Massey Hall. He never set foot in the building again. Instead, between classes, he stayed in the noisy Memorial Union and avoided thumb-fucking his phone.

And he wondered about the people he saw, the people he watched. Wondered what lurked in their pasts. What horrors never forgiven. He couldn't stop himself.

He was forever wondering.

No longer: *What was wrong with Patrick Sanders?*

Now he wondered what was wrong with everyone else.

DAVID H. HENDRICKSON

Full-time professional writer David H. Hendrickson has been a writer for many, many years, not only as a fiction writer, but writing thousands of sports articles. He knows writing. And he knows life.

With Dave, you never know what kind of story you will get, which as editor and fan of his work, I love. This story grabbed me from the title and that opening had me totally hooked, as I tend to be with all of Dave's stories.

Dave's short fiction has appeared in Best American Mystery Stories, Ellery Queen's Mystery Magazine, Heart's Kiss, *and numerous anthologies, including over a half dozen issues of* Fiction River *and just about every issue of this magazine so far. Check it all out at hendricksonwriter.com.*

LITTLE BLUE FUZZY

DAVID H. HENDRICKSON

T hinking he was clicking on his "Sent" email folder when the cursor was actually two lines lower, Mickey DeMarco opened his Spam and found his eyes drawn to one message.

Subject: Unleash the Monster In Your Pants!

Mickey grinned as he leaned back in his swivel chair. How could he not click on that one? It had a ring to it.

Plus, there was the sobering matter of last Saturday night's fiasco with Tina Wolchowski. Mickey still couldn't believe it had happened. Or rather, *hadn't* happened. Forty-one years old, still in the prime of his life, *born* with a boner, and ka-boom, out of nowhere, no lead in the pencil.

And with Tina Wolchowski. Inconceivable.

The next time with Tina—if there ever were a next time, please God let there be a next time—he sure as shit wanted to unleash a monster in his pants.

As his state-of-the-art music system switched from 50 Cent to Fergie, Mickey clicked on the message and...

A tiny image on the page flashed blue and went blank.

Mickey felt a stirring in his crotch, something *extra* down there. His pants bulged. Something, though it sure wasn't the former Old Reliable, was bouncing inside his pants, slamming into the fabric, seeking release.

And using his balls as a fucking trampoline.

Mickey DeMarco stood up and unzipped his fly.

A furry blue streak shot out, caromed off his computer screen, flew up to the ceiling, and plummeted down onto his keyboard.

A tiny, furry, blue creature, looking like the TiVo animated character minus the antennae, spread its arms out wide.

"You called?"

Mickey took a few seconds to respond. "Who the hell are you?"

Barely two inches tall, the creature looked all around, as if puzzled. "I'm The Monster."

Mickey DeMarco peered closer. "You don't look like no monster to me."

Fuzzy scrunched up his face, bared his tiny teeth, and raised his matchstick arms in a menacing pose. He growled.

Mickey looked around the room for hidden cameras and a TV personality lurking in the shadows.

"You ain't no monster."

Fuzzy thrust out his chest. "Who says so?"

Mickey coiled his middle finger against his thumb and flicked the little fuzz-ball to the edge of the desk; he felt soft, more doughboy than monster.

"Hey!" Fuzzy teetered on the precipice, tiny arms wind-milling. "*Hey!*"

Mickey snatched him up and held him out in his palm for a closer look. "I think the word you was looking for was 'help!'"

Fuzzy put his hands on his hips. "It's not in our vocabulary."

"Whose vocabulary?"

"The Monster vocabulary." Fuzzy cocked his head sideways. "You're not too quick on the uptake, you know?"

Mickey thought about crushing the little wiseass, but decided against it. "Yeah, well you're not much of a monster. Only took me one little flick of the finger."

Fuzzy looked taken aback. "You caught me off guard. I thought you were my friend."

"Why'd you think that?"

Fuzzy looked at Mickey as if he were dumb as rocks. "Cause you unleashed me."

Mickey frowned. "Yeah, well, you wasn't what I was expecting. If I'd a-known..."

"What were you expecting? What's wrong with me?"

Mickey scratched himself. "Never mind."

"No, tell me."

"You don't wanna know."

"Yes, I do."

"Well, I was thinking that...that the monster in my pants would be like...you know, a real diamond-cutter."

"A diamond-cutter?"

Was the little shit being deliberately dense? "A boner! A

four-hour, go-to-the-hospital, bang-her-all-night boner. Not a little blue ball of...whatever you're made of."

Fuzzy looked at him with total incomprehension. "What's a boner?"

Mickey stared back. "You really don't know?"

"Am I supposed to?"

The tiny figure waited expectantly.

When some time later Mickey finished his facts-of-life explanation, Fuzzy could only say, "You're kidding, right?"

———

S tanding in front of the bathroom mirror in just his boxers, Mickey DeMarco splashed cologne on his face and underarms.

"Hey, take it easy with that stuff," Fuzzy said, waving his arms wildly atop the sink.

"Women like it. Drives 'em wild."

"You're overdoing it."

"Listen to me, little man. I don't need no help from you when it comes to the ladies. You wouldn't know a pussy from a potato chip."

Fuzzy checked the notes he'd taken while Mickey explained the facts of life. "Would too."

Mickey splashed more cologne on his hands and lathered it on his inner thighs.

"Not down there!" Fuzzy lifted his hands to his throat, gagging. "I won't be able to breathe."

Mickey bent over until his eyes were only a foot from

Fuzzy. "Listen, pal, you ain't going down there. Not now. Not ever. It kinda creeps me out you was there in the first place."

In a blur of bright blue, Fuzzy plummeted to the floor, rebounded, and shot up the opening between Mickey's boxers and his hairy leg. Hanging upside down, Fuzzy poked his tiny head out from the bottom of the shorts. "I can't leave you. We're a team."

Mickey swatted at his boxers as if a spider had crawled up into them, bouncing on the tips of his toes and yelping, only to shoot up an octave when he whacked himself in the balls.

After a time, Mickey's moans and curses subsided.

Fuzzy poked his head out. "Was that an orgasm?"

"Of course not."

He glanced at his notes. "Were you whacking off, also known as spanking the monkey—"

"No!"

"Why is it called *spanking the monkey?*"

"I wasn't spanking the monkey."

"Were you choking the chicken?"

Mickey's anger erupted. "I wasn't choking the chicken or spanking the monkey. I was trying to crush your furry fucking head!"

Fuzzy cocked his head. "Why are you so hostile? I'm only trying to help."

"I don't want your help."

Fuzzy smiled. "I'm The Monster In Your Pants. This is my home. I can't leave now."

Mickey slid the boxers off and dropped them, along with Fuzzy, into a pile. He pulled on another pair, this one with the logo of the New York Jets. But as soon as the elastic touched his waist, a blue streak shot up his leg again.

"You can't stop me," Fuzzy said, his head appearing at the bottom of the boxers. "I'm here to stay."

After a very long time, Mickey asked, "Where down there do you think you're going? 'Cause if you think you're getting near the jewels—"

"Eeew! Gross." Fuzzy wrinkled his nose. "Give me some credit." He pointed inside the shorts. "There's a satin loop here in the back. It has the size and brand name. Makes for a perfect hammock after I shrink a little." He winked. "And you know about shrinkage."

———

An hour later, amidst Café Renaldo's soft buzz of conversation and clatter of silverware against plates, Mickey sipped his wine and tried to focus on the story Katharine Martignetti was telling, something about an English professor having a crush on a female student named Yeats. Mickey guessed it was supposed to be amusing so he smiled in what he thought were the appropriate places, but based on Katherine's reactions, his timing was off. He shoved a mouthful of pasta into his mouth and nodded expectantly.

She was attractive enough, he guessed, as forty-something women went—her ad on the dating website had been surprisingly accurate—but shit on a shingle, she expected him to think too much. Earnest discussions of global warming, politics, and then this story about the English professor. What was this, a first date or a fucking IQ test?

It was tough enough just keeping his mind off what lurked inside his pants. Every time he sat up straight, Fuzzy and his satin hammock dug into his tailbone, forcing him to slouch, a natural enough state for Mickey except that it reminded him once again of the little guy down there in his pants.

"Have you heard a single word I've said?"

Mickey blinked. "Yeah, sure, I was just…ah…"

Fire danced in Katherine Martignetti's eyes, reminding him of a parochial-school nun ready to wrap his knuckles with a ruler. In the silence, he could almost hear the light thwack-thwack against her palm.

The words slipped out like a fart. "See, I got this bulge in my shorts—"

No previous date of Mickey's had ever thrown water in his face. He'd figured that happened only in movies.

Until Katherine Martignetti.

———

Days later, in no mood for another first date with anyone short of Heidi Klum or Marissa Miller, Mickey got together with an old fuck buddy, Janine Brookmeyer. Further into her forties than he was, Janine was a bit chunky for his tastes, with a plain face and sad eyes, but not bad as fuck buddies went.

Within minutes of her stepping into his apartment, they'd gotten right down to business, almost racing to the bedroom. Her top off, she'd loosened his belt, unzipped his fly, and slid her hand down his pants.

Fuzzy shot out in a blue flash. He caromed off Janine's

naked right breast just inside the nipple, crashed into the bedside lamp, and fell onto the nightstand beside the digital clock radio.

Janine shrieked and covered her breasts.

After shaking his head to clear the cobwebs, Fuzzy thrust his hand into the air, tiny index finger extended. "Fear not," he proclaimed, sounding like Underdog in the old cartoon series. "I'm here to save the day."

Janine fell silent. Wide-eyed, she turned to Mickey, who opened his mouth only to close it.

"Who..." Janine began, then faltered. "What..."

"I'm the Monster In Mickey's Pants! And are you going to be one satisfied customer tonight!" Fuzzy glanced around. "Or this afternoon. Whatever the case may be."

Glancing nervously about, Janine gathered her top and bra.

"Whatever you two need," Fuzzy continued, "I'm here to provide. If Mickey can't get it up—" Fuzzy flexed his muscles "—I'll hoist his petard." A confused look crossed his face. "Or whatever it's called." He flashed the broad, confident smile of a used-car salesman. "Your pleasure is guaranteed. Your orgasms will be boundless. Our team is brimming with confidence."

Janine dashed to the bathroom, slammed the door, and locked it.

"What the hell do you think you're doing?" Mickey demanded.

"I can't sit idly by while your love life withers away," Fuzzy said. "I'm taking a proactive approach."

"My love life was fine, thank you very much, until you came along."

Fuzzy eyed him, head cocked.

"Okay," Mickey said. "Except for that one time."

Janine emerged from the bathroom fully clothed. Her thumb and index finger stroked her lips. "How long have you been talking to the...um, the *little guy*?"

Mickey fumbled for words.

Nodding warily, Janine headed for the front door, giving him a wide berth.

"Wait!" Fuzzy called. "Let me explain. Mickey sent for me after he couldn't get it up for Tina Wolchowski."

Janine stopped. "Tina?"

Fuzzy looked back and forth between Mickey and Janine. "He wanted a *monster* in his pants. To pleasure sexy bitches like you."

Janine snatched her purse off the floor and flew out the front door with only a hurried, wide-eyed glance back.

Fuzzy looked perplexed. "Did I say something wrong?"

———

Mickey took charge. He strode to his dresser, a pair of scissors in hand, and slid out the top drawer.

"No more hammocks for you," he said.

With two snips, the satin label fell free in his palm. He reached for another pair of shorts.

A blue streak shot to the pile of underwear. Fuzzy pointed a finger. "I wouldn't do that if I were you."

Mustering his old swagger, Mickey asked, "Why? What're you gonna do?"

"I'll have to hang out somewhere else down there. Some place you might like a lot less."

Icicles slid up and down Mickey's spine. Then anger began to burn deep within. Mickey turned the scissors in his grasp and stabbed at Fuzzy. A blue flash shot off to the right as the scissors pierced several layers of boxers.

Fuzzy materialized on the drawer's edge. "What do you think you're doing?"

"Listen, this is important," Mickey said. "I got another date with Tina Wolchowski this weekend, and you're not gonna screw this one up."

"Last time with her you screwed up all by yourself."

"That's besides the point!" Mickey tried counting to ten, but stopped at three. "You're not gonna spook her like you spooked Janine. She ain't gonna see you. She ain't gonna hear you. 'Cause you ain't even gonna be there."

"I can't leave you."

"Oh, yes, you can, little man."

"I can't! I'm the Monster In Your Pants. That's who I am. It's where I have to be."

Mickey felt like plunging the scissors into his own neck.

"I won't say a word," Fuzzy said. "Trust me. You won't even know I'm there."

When Friday night came, Tina's short, black skirt show-cased wonderfully tanned legs and the promise of more. Her girls jiggled all through dinner, a delicious preview of coming attractions. And on the ride to his apartment, her hands roamed all over him.

Inside his bedroom, Tina got down to a lacey black bra and panties. Mickey moved into her embrace, no problem with Old Reliable this time. No sirree. He had a diamond-cutter for sure, poking against the fabric of Tina's panties. Without a doubt, this time he'd unleashed a monster in his pants.

Mickey groaned. Why had that phrase popped into his head? As his shorts dropped to the floor and a flash of blue streaked to the dresser, he thought of Fuzzy looking on. Fuzzy, whose reaction to Mickey's birds-and-the-bees talk had been, "You're kidding, right?"

Old Reliable began to lose it.

Mickey kissed Tina on the lips and then, removing her bra, moved lower. But instead of seeing those bouncing, beautiful breasts with their large, hardening nipples, his mind's eye saw Fuzzy on top of the dresser, observing with clinical detachment, taking notes like a lab technician decked out in a white lab coat.

Old Reliable faded even more.

Mickey slid his hands inside Tina's panties and found that special spot. She arched her back and tilted her hips. Surefire lead in the pencil on any other day....

But Old Reliable was gone.

Mickey licked her nipples, trying to conceal his failure. He caressed her special spot. Tina was ready, in heat for chrissakes, but...

She didn't say it. Didn't have to. The look in her eyes said it all. *What's wrong?*

She sprang into action, turning her attentions on him, passionate attentions, attentions he would have given his left nut for on any other day. But on this day, Mickey couldn't stop thinking of Fuzzy in his white lab coat watching this failure, shaking his head while scribbling his notes.

After a few minutes, Tina stopped. She tilted her head back and rubbed what must have been a cramp out of her neck.

She didn't need to say a thing. The word she had to be thinking screamed through his own mind.

Again?

What could he say? Once was a fluke; it could happen to any guy. But twice? What was that? A trend? A problem? No, it was a fucking disaster. Surely no other man had problems *twice* performing with Tina Wolchowski.

"I'm sorry." Mickey shook his head. "I don't know what's wrong."

Tina looked at him for a very long time, as if he were some relic in a museum. "It's okay," she whispered.

Face flushed, she gathered her clothes.

———

Mickey had always figured that spammers deserved only slow, painful deaths, but what choice did he have? He couldn't go on like this.

The Internet search took only a few minutes. He entered his credit card information, downloaded the spamming software and database of email accounts, and ran the setup program. After removing his pants and taking a digital photo of Fuzzy relaxing in his satin hammock, Mickey typed:

Subject: Unleash a monster in your pants!

The little furball wasn't a bad guy. He was charming in his own odd way. Mickey just didn't want him in his shorts anymore. Or anywhere else. He'd have to get rid of Fuzzy the same way he got him.

Maybe someone else could put up with the little guy. Soon, someone would get that chance.

Mickey attached the digital photo to the message and feeling only the tiniest sliver of guilt, clicked the mouse.

For a few minutes nothing happened.

Then a blue streak shot from his boxers, flew into his computer screen and disappeared with a loud pop, as if sucked in by a tornado.

Mickey stared at the monitor. He ran his hand over the label in his shorts, smooth and bereft of Fuzzy.

He was free!

Mickey felt Old Reliable growing in his pants. He might never get another chance with Katherine, Janine, and Tina, but there were plenty of other fish in the sea.

Idly he clicked on the Spam folder, prepared to delete all the messages. He wouldn't make that mistake again. But one line caught his attention.

Subject: Nearby Nymphos Want Your Body

Mickey smiled. Was this for real? He doubted it. But one little mouse click wouldn't hurt, would it?

EZEKIEL JAMES BOSTON

Ezekiel James Boston lives in Las Vegas, my new hometown. He has sold stories all over the place. This powerful story might have one of the best character voices I have seen in a long time.

What makes Ezekiel perfect to write Pulphouse *stories is that he has no fear to write about subjects that others in this new world would run screaming from. His skill and his courage are why I hope to have many more Ezekiel James Boston stories in these pages.*

You can find a lot more of his work at a website with the subtitle: Fiction That Doesn't Hide. *ezekieljamesboston.com.*

GUARDING THE BONE CHALICE

EZEKIEL JAMES BOSTON

I'm a junkie and an artist. As such, I both loathe and idolize the Bone Chalice of Anguish.

Bleached white, a foot tall, and six inches in diameter, the chalice is the bottom portion of a long-dead hearty beast with the bone marrow hollowed out for drinking. The rim is filed razor thin to punish the tongue or lips of anyone not being mindful while partaking from the greatness in their hands. Most see it as a black on brown twenty-four-ounce Café Cocoa Java tumbler, but me? I always see the chalice's true shape.

In winter, Orlando's Redstar Arena is one of my favorite places to perform and compose. Their promoters are topnotch, they always fill my riders, and their green rooms are more like luxurious two-bedroom suites than just four walls for performers to wait for their stage call.

The main room has a couple of sofas: a nice hearty black

cloth one for napping and an easy to clean brown leather one for performers with pre-show rituals that might be on the messy side.

Per my rider, the floor is covered with dozens of new mismatched throw rugs so that I can go around barefooted without worry of picking up what someone else left behind. Also, per my rider, the teamsters stopped their banging in the twenty thousand occupancy arena at 11:15 AM so my roadies can start the sound checks and beeping scissor lifts putting up the backdrops and facades.

Right on schedule.

And right about now, my security staff will pretend to confuse a groupie for a delivery person and hand them a replica Jenny, acoustic guitar, and a worn pocket-sized composition notebook to deliver to me.

As much as I hate incense, I've got the nasty nag champa burning because, to activate, the chalice first demands smoke and fire. It'd prefer a roaring Burning Man-like bonfire, but accepts tokens. Even though it's off in the larger room reserved for the star—I have it surrounded by candles in there —it always prefers cold temperatures. So, I got the A/C down at sixty-four.

My brain doesn't register the chill, but my goosebumps and music note tattooed skin does. The tracks on both my arms itch. The groupie is getting closer.

I should be wearing more than just my old loose faded blue jeans cinched on my waste by hemp rope. However, when the chalice starts to whine, I need to feel the vibrations on my sinewy compact chest. While healthy, my body still looks strung out. My mid-back stringy gray hair and sternum long grizzled beard doesn't help.

I rub my baggy front pockets to assure myself that the voodoo queen's straight razors are there.

Lyrics that I started to string together last month in New Orleans come to mind. When I first stole the chalice fifty years ago from Carson—an old bluesman the world has mostly forgotten—songs poured from me. Now, it takes almost a year to pen a new song and the chalice resents me for not lowering my guard so it can be stolen by an unprincipled artist thirsty for fame.

So it can set the city on fire.

To honor Carson, I took on his first name as my stage surname. Much later, he had shared that's I'll know when I have a worthy successor. I never thought I'd want to let it go. Then, I wished I could. Now, I'm numb.

Soft knocks, non-disturbing knocks, tap on my door.

I pad over to the black sofa and plop down on the comfy cushions. "Come in."

A pudgy, dough-faced mid-twenties person with their eyebrows shaved off and eyelashes trimmed down peeks in. Trusting eyes. Then steps in with my loose strapped guitar and comp book. Because of the layers of loose black shirts, baggy black dockers, black combat boots, black gage earring plugs, and unpainted nibbled-short nails, I can't tell if they're a butch woman or a femboy.

"Mr. Carson?" The midrange voice doesn't help nail the gender either, not that it matters. I want to presume female, but I've been wrong before. What matters is that she didn't run off with the replica and also has the comp book in hand.

"Yeah, friend?"

"Um," The lack of confidence and nerves show. As proof that she's supposed to be there, she presents both. "I've got Jenny and Phantom." Bonus points for knowing the name of my comp book.

Still sitting, I extend my hands toward her for Jenny.

She almost runs the guitar to me.

Taking the replica, I sling the strap over my neck and back, and ask, "What's your name?"

"Adrian, sir." Like her voice, her name's no help. She wreaks of cigarette smoke making me want to light up, but her breath is all mint Binaca.

"You must be new to the crew, 'cause there ain't no *misters* or *sirs* 'round here."

Dimples show when she smiled closed mouth. "Sorry, Robert. I mean, friend."

I nod and, strumming scales, I ask, "Well, you gonna sit or do you gotta get back to work?"

"Well, Rob— Friend." She fidgets. "I'm actually a fan."

I raise an eyebrow at her. "A working fan or a fan with time?"

She swallows hard. "With time."

The cigarette smell gets the best of me and I want that throat stinging taste. "Got a smoke?

"Nah." She shook her head. "Trying to quit. Got some mint nic gum though." Her hands are already in her pockets and producing a blister pack before I could say no.

Not wanting it, I stop strumming, accept, and pop it in my mouth. Mint flavoring has come a long way. The thin crunchy casing around the chewing rubber cement-like texture hasn't. I point with Jenny to the far side of the sofa.

Her dimples pit as her round cheeks rise parting her lips to show an awkward and slightly yellowed smile.

I take to picking the slow bluesy notes of my *A Bluesman Knows*.

She says, "That's one of my favs."

"Know the words?"

Her eager nod and doughy face make her look like a juvenile. I know security checked her ID, so she's at least twenty-one, but right then I almost ask.

I bring the tempo up to normal. "Let's hear it, then."

"What?" Her cheeks redden. "Oh, no. You don't want that. I can't sing."

"Neither can I." I wink. "That's why I speak my lyrics. I'm known to hold a note or two hostage, but singing ain't my thing either."

She just shakes her head.

I cycle back to the opening notes. "It's just you and me, friend." Sadly, I've already forgotten her name. Didn't really put any effort into remembering it. Decades of dozens of nights each year of moments just like this have jaded me. Most chicken out. I play them a few songs and then ask them to leave.

When the lyrics are supposed to start, she shakes her head again.

I cycle back to the opening notes and give her my most encouraging smile. "Last chance, buttercup. If you don't, I will. As thanks. You know, for delivering these."

She shakes her head.

"'Kay then." Getting to where the lyrics come in, I tongue the gum into my cheek and close my eyes.

She says, *"In Naw'lins—"*

I nod appreciatively at the lyrics and keep my mouth shut.

Her voice lilts and cracks as she continues. *"An old risen voodoo woman gave me a crooked knowing grin."*

Vibrations from the other room tingle my chest. Sensing what's coming, the chalice whines.

She continues, *"She said, 'You may got love on the inside, child, but the devil, he on your skin.'"*

Looking at her might spook her. So, I keep my eyes closed, play the music, and enjoy the chalice whining for her to stop.

———

The Bone Chalice of Anguish has probably had many other—and more accurately nefarious—names through time. Names I don't know and names bluesman Carson never hinted at. The only names that are famous are the cities the chalice burned and a rare few who failed to keep their ego in check: most notably Emperor Nero.

From my own experience, I know the chalice digs hooks into creatives. Giving inspiration for smoke and fire. For blood and death. Incense used to be enough to keep me in the zone and I know the chalice is getting to me as I try to pen my last great tune because I've taken to lighting candles around it.

Buttercup reciting my lyrics fills me with a sense of pride and I open my eyes while stringing songs together, waiting for her to hear the increasing volume of the whining chalice herself. Knowing that my music will live on in her, I don't mind eventually being forgotten.

As she starts to roll up her sleeves, I glance over at the thermostat. It's still at sixty-four. She's feeling the chalice's heat. If she doesn't hear it, she'll start to soon smell the smoke that—after a couple of hours of her reciting my lyrics—is starting to make the room hazy for me.

The scissor lifts have stopped, but the sound checks continue. In the moment, she's oblivious to it all.

I stifle a cough and recall Carson doing the same fifty years ago. Back then, I hadn't experienced the chalice like he had and buttercup was as blissfully ignorant as I had been in Carson's dressing room.

Rotating her arms like I often did while proforming, the insides of each of her hairless arms has scores of healed over cuts. A few deep enough that she'd probably been hospitalized.

I glance to my years-closed, itching tracks. They're puckered open like tiny barnacles ready to feed. Begging for a fix that'll numb me to the chalice's adverse effects.

We're all troubled.

A tendril of black smoke tipped with an ill-willed orange incense coal writhes from the other room. Seeking out its annoyance, it kinks and snakes toward buttercup's back.

I want to warn her, but she needs to feel it. The tiny brand on the back of my neck seers. I grimace and keep strumming. Keep her distracted.

She yips when it licks her.

My entire spine lights with that same pain. It's the chalice burning me from within for not protecting it.

Before she can turn, the smoke dissipates and she's left trying to knock the ember from the base of her neck.

It'll cool, but it'll never go away. Not even in the slightest.

Jumping up and searching the sofa, she asks, "What was that?"

As if I don't know, I ask, "What was what?"

Her hands go to the back of her neck. "Something bit me."

It wasn't a bite. I collect my gray hair and move it sideways for her to see my similar bump. "Oh, it got me, too. Earlier." I don't tell her *fifty years* earlier.

She points to the star's dressing room. "I think it flew back in there."

"In there?" I feel like an ass as I get up to search for what I know did it. She's only half right. The menace returned to the chalice, the thick smoke that only I could see—for now— pooled against the ceiling.

Standing, I sling the guitar behind me and slip my hands into my pockets and ball my fists around the straight razors to cut the candles if need be. I head toward the dressing room. The faint whiff of her burnt flesh punches sweetly into my nose like a single rose. It's the chalice's promise of a field of roses—a city of roses—if I were to just turn it loose. That, more than anything, sets my resolve.

She's right behind me. "Is it smokey in here?"

Not being a hundred percent truthful, I say, "A little." If the arena staff opened the green room door, they'd probably think that we'd been vaping.

The nag champa incense is stronger in the stars room. Fruitlessly, trying to choke me out, the chalice thickens the nasty taste in my mouth.

I cough the smoke out.

The center of the east wall in the star's dressing room has a light-rimmed, full-length mirror separating two makeup stations with counters and smaller light-rimmed mirrors. Surrounded by five tall red thin candles that still look freshly lit, the bone chalice sits on the left counter. One of the three incense sticks behind it is missing its ember.

Like whatever had bit her had gone into the bathroom, I turn that way.

She asks, "What's *that?*"

I glance to her and my gaze follows her point to the chalice. "History." I say, "Ancient and old." As though that was enough, I release the razors, and sling the replica in front of me. "You play?"

"No." She steps back like it might burn her, too. "Not at all."

Trying to encourage her, I place my fingers on a D chord. "This—" I strum. "Is a simple D chord."

"Simple for you, maybe." She's apprehensive.

"Simple." I insist, "For anyone who tries." I slip the strap from over my neck and extend the replica. "And I do mean anyone."

She eyes me. "You can tell me about a D chord," Her gaze goes back to the chalice. "But you can't tell me about that?"

"Well—" I take a step toward her. "Play a D chord and I'll tell you somethin'."

Sensing danger, or maybe the years of struggle ahead of her, she steps back. "I'm going to go."

Shit. "'Kay." I nod. No one living understands her apprehension as much as I do. For the first few years, I had wished that I had ran away when my instincts told me to.

I keep the guitar extended toward her. "You know where the door is, buttercup. You have a great story to share with your friends and a couple of songs to write."

"Songs?" She sneered confusion. "I'm not a song writer. I'm not even a poet."

Feeling tired, I smile at her. I don't know how much longer I'll be able to resist the chalice's destructive desires if she goes, but I can't make her sign up for this.

On me like a hound on a leg, the chalice makes the candles flicker and a few more words of my next song comes to me. I make a mental note for my manager to add a couple more candles to my rider.

She blinks amazement at the chalice. "I…" She trails off.

I know.

From my first flicker, I had almost an album's worth of lyrics about my struggle against, and numerous losses to, heroine. I didn't known that my herculean strength to kick the habit had been aided by the chalice. The strong addictive want for the drug supplanted by just a kiss of a request to know more about the chalice.

Her gaze ranged the guitar strings like a mouse scanning for a prowling cat. "You'll tell me more if I play a D."

"Some." I don't lie. "I'll tell you some." I cut my eyes to the door and stare at the wall where the door out of the green room is. "But there's always leaving." Hoping she can, but praying her curiosity won't let her, I say, "And you can leave if you want to."

Her gaze goes to my tracks, then to the cuts on her arms.
She steps back.

Shit.

L ike searing brands, poems about depression, abuse, and
self-harm blaze in the thick smoke. Next to them, as
though translated from old biblical text into something
common people could relate to, the song version: verses,
choruses, bridges, and—on some—intros and outros.

They're great songs. The kind of tunes that'll get untold
thousands through rough time. Sparking from the lyrics,
music notes, chords, full song sheets that'd best accompany
the tune. Whole songs there in the air. They're seared in my
mind and I could pen them, but they aren't mine to share with
the world. She could easily be this generation's Dylan or Petty.

A poem about me fades from view, but I catch the first two
long lines.

*He wore blue jeans and a smile. And I could tell that it'd been a
while, since he rested without worry. His sad eyes scold me and told
me that the miles stack up, buttercup, and the years and faces get
blurry.*

I'd love to hear her recite the entire poem.

The bouquet of her burn is in my nose and lungs as I—and
her songs—follow her to the door. A floor washing machine
whrrrs out there and I stop in the middle of the room.

The temperature's still at sixty-four. I eye one of her songs
about running away from an abusive foster home only to be

returned by the cops for more abuse. Starting the simple 6/4-time signature, I strum four chords D, A, Bm, G to her tune.

Humming it, she still leaves and closes the door behind her.

Playing, I rush to the door and open it during a brief lull. Piney disinfectant seeps in as the strong smoke that only I can see billows out, scattering buttercup's poems, lyrics, and sheet music.

The guy riding the floor washer cuts it off and leans on the little steering wheel to listen.

Stepping back into the room, I switch from the 6/4 into the complex 6/8-time signature of her chorus.

I hear her voice trailing away down the hall. *"I can run away, but I can't get away. And now I have to pay because I have to stay."*

Feeling it—deeply because of my connection to the chalice —I do my best to back her up, both physically and in singing.

I echo, *"Have to stay."*

The volume of her speak-singing drops off. She must've turned a corner.

Wishing that I had an electric guitar, amp, and speaker, I play the repeated chorus louder and—where timed—called out, "Have to stay."

I stop strumming.

The guy on the riding floor washer drives by giving me a thumbs up. "Sounding good, Mr. Carson."

"Thanks, friend." It's hollow, but I say it. I close the door and, playing for myself, I ease down onto the cloth sofa and— tracks itching with familiar want—pick the music back up to play it to completion.

Leaning my head back, I resist looking at my tracks.

Like in the past, when I acted against the chalice, it no longer lets me ignore the cold. The chill plays on the tiny mouths that I refuse to look at. They lip:

Hungry

Want

Feed us.

Like a bad penny, an oh too familiar knocking to the sound of Marilyn Manson's *I Don't Like the Drugs* starting lyrics raps my door. I don't know how Jackson, my old supplier always knows when to show up with junk for me, but he does. And he always uses the same damn knock.

I had heard that he died. I had hoped that he had dead.

Jackson's deep voice resonates through the door. "Need a little something to take the edge off?" He sings like a peanut vendor at a baseball game. "I've got some ninety-five percent and neeeeedles."

Shaking my head, I yell, "Go away!"

The door opens and Jackson leans in with that big-toothed grin that promises a six-week bender and another trip to rehab if my luck holds out.

Shit, I didn't lock it. I should've locked it.

He says, "Well, if my best customer insists that I come in…" He's wearing tie-dyed sweats with a yellow happy face on the chest.

Already unhooking the guitar strap to use it to tie off, I say, "I said *go away*, Jackson."

He chuckles. "In a minute."

Tied-off, I lean my head back again and resist the overpowering sensation to scratch my tracks. If I do, they'll bite me. The only soothing they want comes through a needle.

"Excuse me." Buttercup's voice enters the room.

Jackson says, "Who'dis?"

I glance.

Buttercup is pushing Jackson out. She says, "A friend."

Looking at me over her head as he backsteps, Jackson says, "I'll be right out here once you're done with this scrumptious, plumptious groupie."

Buttercup slams the door and locks it. Turning, she says, *"The pain is the only thing I can control. It's only when I'm cut open that I feel whole."*

The chalice whines.

My tracks cry with it.

Her lyrics touch me and I want her help, but am shaking my head at her. "He's got ninety-five percent."

She waggles the small comp book. "And your music is pure. Uncut."

Corny. So horribly corny. I sigh. Wanting the drugs more than my comp book that I have memorize, I don't untie. I sit up.

Waving her away, I say, "Keep it. Souvenir."

Walking over, she tosses it on the leather sofa. "I don't want *that*."

Having a feeling that she's coming over for my jeans, I ask, "What do you want, then?"

She plops down next to me. "Friend." Her minty breath is warm against my chilled skin. Instead of undoing my pants, she undoes the guitar strap, and say, *"Chords."*

M y spine lights with pain as she strums D, A, Bm, G. Where I've grown near impotent to combat the chalice, each one of her chords beats back the black smoke. It builds up at the star dressing room, but cannot come further as she clumsily strums her way through her *Can't Get Away* song. Her fingering improves on her second time through and, when her minty voice speaks the lyrics, the smoke lessens, the chalice whimpers, and my spine cools.

Staring off into the air, her voice gains confidence as she switches up the chords to transition into her *Cut Open* song. Before she finishes, the air in the star's dressing room is clear. There's not even a whiff of the nasty nag champa. My tracks are still open, but instead of mouths, they're redden sores as though I've used each of them too many times.

This pain I know.

This pain is all too familiar.

This pain is manageable and within my threshold.

Leaving her strumming on the sofa, I peer into the star's dressing room. The candles around the chalice are out and the incense sticks are half unused and snuffed.

If her time with me will be anything like my time with Carson, she'll spend just about a year with me before she realizes that I'm sneaking time with the chalice. That's when she'll steal it and scram.

Focusing on tonight, I sit myself back down on the cloth sofa away from her so that I can stretch out a bit. As she plays and speaks her lyrics, I plan out the conversation that'll get her to come on stage with me. I can't play with my sores reawakened and, thinking it's just about the guitar, she'll come just to play.

And, on stage, I'll have her play *Can't Get Away* for me, which the crowd will love.

Strumming, she tells me that her stage name will be Buttercup Roberts and I know—regardless of how I'll fade into obscurity—that the chalice will be in good hands.

ROBERT JESCHONEK

Robert Jeschonek continues his streak of being in every issue of this magazine.

The reason Robert has this streak is simply because his stories are often just perfect Pulphouse stories. Take this story, for example. Heck, just look at the title and you will know what I mean, and the story lives up to the title.

Robert's stories have appeared in dozens of magazines and he has published dozens of novels as well. He has even worked for DC Comics and early in his career sold me a couple stories when I was editing for Star Trek at Pocket Books. He seems to be able to do it all. And to see all the amazing projects he has done, check out his website at robertjeschonek.com.

THE REALM THAT DIDN'T SUCK

ROBERT JESCHONEK

White clouds. *Blue sky. Yellow sun.*

Even as I fall, flailing, into the latest in a long line of realms, those are the first things I notice. And even though I'm falling fast, worrying about where and how hard I'll come down, a coherent thought flashes through my mind.

I like this place already.

Then *crack*, I'm crashing through a canopy of green and brown, a heartbeat away from whatever hard landing awaits me. A heartbeat away, maybe, from the *death* of me.

But no. Instead of pancaking on solid ground, I splash down in icy water. The breath is knocked out of me, I sink deep, but I survive.

It's a good thing I'm not the woman I used to be. *Original* Mia couldn't have stayed under for long with no air. But *this* Mia's another story.

Ten thousand stories, actually.

Midway through my plunge, my legs transform, melting

into a kind of fish tail. Immediately, I thrash that tail hard, slowing my fall—then stopping it altogether.

Looking around through my cloud of glowing red hair, I become aware of eyes peering at my slender body from the emerald murk. Squinting, I glimpse the face of an underwater creature before it wriggles off into the shadows...and I'm stunned. Was it my imagination, or did that thing actually look like a *fish* from back home? From Original Mia's starting point?

Frowning, I swim my way toward the light.

When I break the surface, gasping, the world opens up around me. My tail keeps me afloat as I take it all in—a forest of trees with brown trunks and green leaves, set against that lovely blue sky with white clouds above, all of it reflected in the rippling surface of the lake below.

All of which just makes me think, *Holy shit.* As in, *Holy shit, I never thought I'd see someplace like* this *again.*

I laugh, because it's wonderful, a miracle—and then I swim for shore. All the while, I keep waiting for the other shoe to drop, because as I've learned again and again (*and again*) in my many travels...

Appearances can be deceiving.

When I reach the shallows, I undo the fish tail, giving myself human legs again. My bare feet sink into the muddy bottom as I wade through the water—more brown here than green—and up onto the grassy beach.

Then, I throw myself down on my back and rest, gazing up at the bright blue sky. It's the first of that color I've seen since leaving home, ten thousand worlds ago (or more), and so many years ago I've lost track.

It makes me want to cry because I've missed it so much. Because, also, I wasn't sure until now, as changed as I am, if I *could* still miss it like I do.

It's funny how much of a relief that is, since all I wanted in the beginning was to get away from it. But I soon discovered that all the other realms with all the other skies were never as perfect as the blue sky of home.

You can take your purple skies, green skies, striped skies, musical skies, diamond skies, et cetera and shove them up your ass. Do the same for all the realms under them in what I call the *Suckyverse* (because that's what they all are, take it from me—*sucky*).

But enough of this lying around. Time to get back to the hunt, the whole reason I'm here.

Sitting up, I use the fire magic in my belly to heat my skin, lighting it up cherry red and instantly drying myself and my clothes, such as they are. The white peasant's blouse and brown ankle-length skirt are ill-fitting, the best I could scare up in the last realm—yet another dragon-infested dump lousy with knights and gnomes a-questing.

"That's better." The crimson glow fades from my glittering marble skin—a creamy base veined with whorls of black and ruby. It's not my natural color or choice, just a side effect of some of the dumbass realms I've dived into.

I get to my feet, wondering what surprises this new realm will bring—what *changes*. Wondering how badly this place will end up *sucking* in the end, because they always do.

That's when I feel something or someone watching me.

Without turning, I open the eye in the back of my head

(another gift from another sucky world) and have a look. What I see is enough to make my heart flutter.

Though every realm I've been to has had its beasts, I've not seen one of *these*, quite like this, in any other...except one.

A *deer*. A beautiful, unaltered, white-tailed *doe*.

I catch my breath, marveling at the sight of it. Wondering how it's possible to find one here, when the only other place I've seen one just like it...

Is *home*.

Which raises a question. Is it possible? After all the places I've been, all the *shitmares* I've lived through, could my quarry —my *love*—have somehow led me back to where I *started*? Could *this* be...*home*?

Suddenly, the doe's ears twitch, and it leaps away, gone like a tawny whisper in the lush green brush.

I look around for whatever spooked it, instinctively saying the name of the one I followed to get here. "Will?" My voice is touched with hope, though I know how unlikely it is that he might be here. The last time I saw him in the flesh was ten thousand realms ago (or more)...though he leaves a message for me in every realm I visit.

Nothing here yet, though. I look, and listen, and smell, and no sign of him comes back to me. I *know* he traveled this way, I followed his trail through the Suckyverse (which *he* taught me how to do, by the way)...but whatever he might have left for me remains hidden.

Though I wonder. If this *is* home after all, with magicks so much dimmer than the multitude of other realms, would he even *leave* a sign for me to find?

Still getting my bearings, I pick my way along the shore to

a ragged path that might have been worn through the brush by the deer and her friends. I follow it, winding away from the water and into the denser cover of the forest.

Snapping twigs tickle my feet as I walk, and rocks jab from the dusty ground—but my skin never breaks and never will. Spell after spell has toughened it, making it nearly impenetrable. My bones and organs, likewise, are much changed, mystically braced and laced with power from a thousand thundering realms...paid for with this bit or that of trickery, honest work, or my mortal soul.

I take another step, and something tiny scurries across a sunbeam in my path. Brown and white striped fur, erect tail, flickering legs...*I'll be damned.*

Was that a *chipmunk?*

The beat of my heart picks up, and I quicken my step. All these similarities to home, they're adding up...but I can't get too excited. The realms are rife with tomfoolery and bullshit. Why do you think they *suck* so much?

That isn't to say I can't enjoy the beauty until the façade tears away. Those shafts of sunlight, streaming through the fluttering green canopy...the sweet, sweet smell of bark and brush and loam, weaving in the crisp, fresh air...and that high, piping skirl—is that *birdsong*, yes it's *birdsong*—it's straight out of a dream, a thousand thousand dreams and memory fragments...a hundred thousand longings.

Shivers of joy run down my spine, setting the vertebrae (altered) to ringing like a choir of bells. Nothing in the realms of endless diadems or dancing gardens or untold mindful rainbows or infinite unfolding parasols can compare to the simple glory in which I find myself.

And I know, even if this sense of familiarity and welcome is limited to this single lovely wood, that there is more joy to come. Because somewhere, as always, in every realm I've been to, there is a message from beloved Will. He always speaks to me, always believes I'm coming after him, though he has no way of knowing for sure that I'll follow.

The message, whatever its form, whatever its medium, is always the same: *I love you, Mia.*

I love you, Will. If I were the one leaving the message, that's how it would read.

Would I always believe, without any proof, that he would see it? That he would never give up his pursuit, and the messages would never be for nothing?

I like to think so, yes. I like to think our love is *that* strong and then some.

The thought of him makes me prick up my ears, open all of my eyes (there are seven) and inhale more deeply in search of his sign. No wonder I'm extra sensitive when a tiny black bug circles around and lands on my wrist.

How many such horseflies did I swat in younger years back home? Yet now, watching the little bastard rub his legs together, I'm delighted. I never thought I'd see one like this again—one that isn't eight feet tall or chanting obscenities or riding a giant centipede with the head of a ghost wizard spewing out acid. He's a plain and simple fly, a little piece of paradise, and I'm sad to see him spring off when I raise my arm for a closer look.

I follow his swerving, crisscross course as if he's Will leading me through the Suckyverse—with about as much chance of catching up. He leads me up a hill where the trees and brush start to thin. Instead of shafts of sunlight dappling the forest floor, falls of brightness cascade down through the sparser overgrowth.

When at last I emerge from the treeline at the edge of a grassy clearing, I bask and stretch in the undiluted warmth and light. My neon red hair curls and glows brighter; the light of *any* sun—blue, brown, speckled pink and green, goat's head, lollipop, cat's eye—will give it a boost...but guess what, *yellow* gives it a downright *orgasm.*

As my eyes adjust to the light, I scan the space before me— the size of a baseball diamond, encircled mostly by trees, open at the far end. There, in the distance, I glimpse something—a peak? A steeple? Something that *might* be manmade (*Will*-made), though I can't tell for sure from here.

Starting forward through the knee-high grass, I wonder what sign or signal Will has left for me this time. It's always something different.

Two realms ago, for instance, in the world of the whale-phants' graveyard, he left a giant ossuary of porcelain whale-phant bone with his message spelled out in massive rills of tusk and horn. It was a marvel (how did he *do* that?) and most importantly, it stood the test of time.

Because it *had* to. Because I didn't get to *see* it for a *thousand years* after it was built.

That's the whole problem with our travel—the *curse* of it. Will and I are forever out of sync.

Ten thousand realms (or more) ago, I stumbled at the first gateway, so we left our starting point seconds apart. In the Suckyverse, however, seconds can add up to years, decades, centuries, or more, depending on your destination.

So I've been chasing him ever since, constantly trying to catch up with him. And every time I follow his trail to another realm, he's already gone from it. He *has* to be. He's not immortal; if he waited around in one place, and I didn't come through the gateway for a hundred years or more, he'd be dead before I got there.

And so our only shot at a reunion is *this*: to keep running. To keep the faith. To hope that next time, maybe *next time*, the lag between his arrival and mine will only be hours or days instead of decades.

The soft grass brushes my legs as I stride through the clearing, eyes trained on what I keep hoping is a Will-made point up ahead. I'm distracted only briefly by a butterfly—*a butterfly!*—as it swirls past on lacy wings of black and umber. I grin and clap my hands like a child as it dances away on the warm breeze, tangibly unremarkable and all the more amazing because of it.

I just hope, if a simple butterfly can make me this giddy, that I don't freak out *too much* when I get to whatever beckons over yonder.

Mission accomplished. As I close in, and the object comes into focus, I'm too totally stunned to giggle. Halfway there, in fact, I stop and stare. My right hand twitches involuntarily, just about making the sign of the cross in pious wonder.

"Will." I whisper the word like a fanatic. He's not there, of course—but he *was*.

And to me, given our synchronization issues, that's the next best thing to a solid week of lovemaking.

The initial shock fades, and I hurry toward it—toward the

prize I know he left for me. The priceless, beautiful *treasure* he somehow conjured on the spot.

The ladder.

I'm hesitant to touch it at first, and not because it looks rickety enough to collapse under the weight of a harsh word. Not because it looks gnarled and spindly as an old crone's bones, barely wound together by garlands of frilly flowers.

The truth is, that's exactly how it looked back then, on that mountain in Nepal, and Will and I climbed it anyway. We climbed it during a grand astrological alignment, chanting from mystic Tibetan, Mayan, Celtic, Egyptian, and Indian scrolls, bodies painted with charms and balms and sigils out of a dozen arcane texts dearly come by.

When his foot left the top rung, he was gone like a whispered word. After the briefest, fateful stumble, so was I.

Many worlds and much time later, my hand snakes out and touches the knobby wood, the pale flowers. *Perfect. No portal into the Suckyverse on top, but otherwise no difference. It could be the original item, for all I know.*

Though seeing it makes me doubt that I've come home. There's no way this place is Nepal. More likely it's some other realm, and the ladder's just a copy.

But why go to the trouble of putting it here? It's a symbol of our separation, not our love, after all.

If Will had wanted to remind me of good times, he could have recreated any of a slew of other gateways—the minor portals he took me through during training jaunts before the big leap into the Suckyverse. That altar deep in the jungle of Guyana, for example, that shot us into a world of feathered leopards with gods for claws. Or the cave pool on the distant island of Tristan da Cunha that took us to a kingdom of surreal faceless weirdos in the gut of a giant frog. Or the hole under the floorboards in the cabin in Alaska that sent us into a land where every dream takes on a life of its own.

Those were the best of times for me, not *these*. Back when Will was someone I'd met in pagan circles, someone who could take me far from the ugly little black magic sex ring I'd gotten mixed up in—though just *how* far, I never imagined. Then the *wonder* of it as he taught me how to find and open the doorways on my own...and the joy of traveling by his side, of opening the love between us as we opened uncharted worlds and dreamed of frontiers grander still. The intensity of those secret adventures that we shared forged an unbreakable bond between us unlike any I've ever known.

So why *this* as a message? And for that matter...why *that*?

Fifty feet beyond the ladder, there's a door—an actual, freestanding red *door* with knob and hinges in a white frame —obscured until now by its angle along the scalloped treeline.

"What the hell?" Eyes narrowed, I head for it. It's been a while since he's left me a *puzzle* message to figure out.

As I get closer, I reach out with all my senses, feeling around for an actual portal or rift, which would figure. Finding nothing of the sort, I'm left to wonder—why is this here? Unlike the ladder, it's not at all familiar.

Again, I hesitate to touch it. And I almost let go when my fingers wrap around the cool brass doorknob—because something *happens*.

The second I take hold of that doorknob, I hear distant *music*...not music like the singing of conflicted dragon-virgins or the humming of pixie pistols at 20 fluttering paces or the strumming of every sphere and sinew in a one-man universe.

More like the music of *home*. Music to my *ears*.

The music of the rock band *Heart*, after all these years.

"Holy shit." I push the door open and step through. There's no magic portal involved, I could just walk around...but this seems more in the spirit of things.

On the other side, I follow the music to the crest of a hill. Looking down, I see one of the oddest sights I've come across in all the realms—not a castle or dragon's lair or village but a kind of triangular *strip mall* in a field.

The mall has colorful storefronts on all three sides, facing outward, and a big white gazebo in a courtyard in the middle. It's like something I might see at home...except there's no parking, just green grass swaying all around.

Intrigued, I start down the hill. "What's the deal here, Will?" It's the first time he's left me a strip mall, and I'm dying to find out why.

I reach the bottom and jog across the field. Squinting with all my forward-facing eyes, I make out more details—and excitement kicks in.

My jog becomes a run, and the music gets louder. "Dog and Butterfly" is one of my favorites.

I recognize those storefronts.

Single-minded as a guided missile, I race toward them. The colors and signage are intimately familiar, though I haven't seen any such places since entering the Suckyverse.

The first one I head for is the coffee place. Its mermaid emblem beams at me from a glowing disk in the window, framed by deep green sills and awnings.

I jump up and down in front of the place and laugh out loud. It's a *perfect* replica of a place I *love*.

Then I go for the door, which thank God isn't locked.

Inside, it looks just like the one on my block back home—low lighting, comfy chairs, magazine-strewn tables. It *smells* the same, too, the air rich with brewed coffee and steamed milk...though there isn't a soul in sight.

Could it be?

Eyes wide (all of them), I rush to the counter. There are paper cups, lidded, at the pickup station (all ventis), and all have the same thing scrawled on the side in black marker:

Mia.

I grab one like it's trying to get away...and it is *hot*. Best of all, it smells like coffee—and something else.

I raise the cup to my nose, close my eyes, and inhale deeply. Is that...could it be...?

"Oh, yes!" I take a sip without further delay. The hot liquid rolls into my mouth, sending every (enhanced) taste bud singing its own variation on the *Hallelujah Chorus*. Because *yes*, that's *caramel* in there.

And that's my favorite hot beverage of all time, a *caramel macchiato*.

That first taste tells me everything I need to know. There's no poison in the cup, no drug or curse—just rich, bitter coffee, foamy cream, sweet vanilla, and buttery caramel.

It's perfect, just like I remember. It doesn't even suck a little, unlike most of the shitty grogs, sour wines, spoiled milks, and drain cleaner moonshines I've come across in hopping between realms.

"Thank you!" Of course Will can't hear me, he's gone, but I say it anyway. "Thank you so much, Will! This is *great!*"

Whatever this realm is, it just keeps getting better. It might not be home, but it's home's greatest hits...and I'm not done exploring yet.

Cradling the macchiato in both hands, I leave the coffee shop and turn right. My heart's pounding, because I remember what storefront is there.

If it's anything like the coffee shop, I have a real treat in store for me.

Looking at the front window, I get a good feeling. The trim and signage are mostly bright red with glittering gilt flourishes and lettering, just like my favorite restaurant back home.

Bhagavad Eat-a. Just the name makes me smile. Now if only there's something inside that makes me smile even more.

Bingo! When I open the door (bell jingling) and walk in, I see a table in the middle of the dining room covered with plates of steaming food. There's even a place card with my name on it in front of the single chair: *Mia*.

As soon as I see that spread, my stomach growls. How long has it been since I've had Indian food?

Too freakin' long.

As in the coffee shop, there isn't another person in sight—and I couldn't care less. The smell of Indian spices drives me crazy. The sight of my favorite dish—chicken tikka masala—strips away my self-control.

"Oh, Will." I put down the caramel macchiato and sit at the loaded table. "This looks heavenly." Gingerly, I sniff at the chicken, magically testing for contaminants. I do the same for the dosa, naan, mango lassi drink, and gulab jamun dessert.

Then, I nod. Calmly pick up a fork.

And attack what's on the table like a mongoose going after a live cobra salad.

By the time I'm done, there's hardly a crumb left on the table. I lean back in the chair, patting my stomach and smiling with woozy satisfaction.

"You've outdone yourself, Will." I wish he could hear the compliment. "That was the best meal I've had since *ever.*"

Overall, this is the best *message* since ever—though I find myself wondering why it's so different from all the rest I've seen. When it comes to this puzzle, I don't feel like I'm seeing the whole picture.

So I guess I ought to keep opening doors until I do.

Leaving Bhagavad Eat-a, I wander around the corner to the next storefront, which happens to be a recreation of my all-time favorite gelato shop, Spumoni-Free Zone.

Like the version back home, the color scheme here is red, white, and green. Like the first two places in the strip mall, it's deserted...but stocked with goodies for yours truly.

The display case is full of colorful gelatos, brightly lit—and a triple-scoop dish of my favorite, *zabaione,* on the counter with my name on it.

I'm pretty full, but there's no way I'll turn my nose up at that *zabaione.* Like the macchiato and Indian food, I haven't had it since leaving home.

I take it with me as I tour the rest of the mall, excavating the sweet, pale cream with a tiny blue plastic gelato spoon. Each bite is more heavenly than the last.

The rest of the tenants of the strip mall are like that too, for me: heavenly. One after another, I gape at storefronts out of my past—my favorite pizza place, clothing shop, shoe store, bookstore, bar, and more. All of them are just as I remember, perfect in every detail...except one.

There's not another human soul in sight.

I see birds, rabbits, and squirrels here and there—all outside—but no people. As for a message, I guess it should be obvious: this is all a gesture of love from him to me...but something seems off.

By the time I get to a bubble tea shop, and a cold cup of my favorite flavor (taro) is waiting with my name on it, I'm full-on questioning the miracle. The Suckyverse is lousy with magic, and Will's a master of employing it in elaborate romantic gestures...but I can't imagine how he rigged this place to work like it does. It's a *masterpiece*.

How long did it take to set it all up? How the hell long was he *here*, anyway, before moving on?

Maybe I can get a clue from his escape route. Sometimes, reading the magical energy of a gateway can tell you things, like how long ago it was last used.

Closing my eyes, I reach out with my mind like he taught me, feeling for a portal to the next place. I probe far and wide, extending my magically enhanced senses in all directions, groping for a doorway.

And I find nothing.

My eyes snap open. There are no words for the level of shock I feel.

That can't be right.

I try again, focusing harder. Again, I find nothing. Even the gateway that brought me here has gone dark.

"Oh my God." My heart slams like a wrecking ball in my chest. "*There's no way out.*"

It doesn't seem possible. The one good thing about the Suckyverse is that there's *always* a way out—*more* than one, usually. If you don't like the current realm, maybe the next one will be better (though more often than not, it's *worse*). I've never even *heard* of a dead end realm.

It doesn't seem natural. So maybe, I realize, it *isn't*. Maybe it's a...

Suddenly, the sky goes dark. There's no twilight, no gradual transition; it's as if a switch has been flipped. One minute, it's bright blue and sunny, and the next, it's starry and black.

Just as suddenly, my blood turns cold. I think I've solved the puzzle.

The pieces fit. *This* is why there's been no actual message from Will. *This* is why a parade of my favorite things has been trotted out before me. *This* is why all the exits have been shut, if ever they were open to begin with.

"It's a *trap*." Even possessing the power to warm myself from within, I shiver against the icy truth of it. "A trap for *me*."

But set by whom? And to what end?

I call up the magic within me, putting my altered body into a battle configuration. My tough marbled skin sprouts spines, and my glowing red hair bursts into flame. My breath catches fire, too, and my eyes flash with searing red laser-like light. My right arm becomes a razor-sharp scythe, and my left arm transforms into a shield.

Whoever's coming to get me, *let them try. Half* my enhancements won't even be *visible* to an enemy until it's *too late.* How the hell do you think I've survived the Suckyverse all this time?

"Who are you?" I howl at the heavens as I storm around the storefronts. All at once, they light up from within. "What do you *want* from me?"

The wind picks up. Heart keeps playing; it's "Barracuda" now. Otherwise, I get no reply.

My mind races, straining to fill in the blanks. Other that Will, who or what could *do* all this? Construct these elaborate replicas of places back home, complete with food, drink, and merchandise customized to suit me? It must have taken some masterful conjuring, to say the least.

Not to mention, it took some intimate knowledge of *me.* Whoever did this knew enough about my favorite things and places to create a virtual paradise with my name on it, literally. Did they read my mind when I got here? Or did the information come from *someone else?*

Just then, it hits me. Maybe there's a reason Will didn't leave me a message on his way out. After all, there's *no way out.*

"He's here, isn't he?" The words burst from me like the searing red beams I shoot from my eyes to slash at the sky for impact. "You *took* him!"

The ground rumbles under my feet. Whoever did this, are they *coming?* Am I finally drawing them out?

"Where *is* he? What have you *done* with him?" Wondering where to look for Will, I remember the view from the top of the hill—the gazebo in the central courtyard of the strip mall.

I'll need to go through one of the shops to get there, so I open the nearest door and march inside, flaming tresses singeing the casement on the way. I find myself in a copy of my favorite sushi bar back home—Life Rolls—but I sweep past the trays of tender morsels without missing a step. I'm through the back door in nothing flat...and then I freeze.

Between me and the gazebo, the grassy central courtyard is studded with gray tubes of varying size. Some are inches in diameter, some a foot or more, and all are stuck in the ground, pointing straight up.

The tubes are connected by a network of lines laid out on the ground between them. I wonder if I might trip something by walking over it—but if Will's in the gazebo, do I have another choice?

"Will?" I call out across the courtyard, and no one answers. Maybe the music's too loud; it's coming from speakers arrayed around the roof of the gazebo, hung just under the overhang.

"Will?" I amplify my voice by magical means and try again, making it roar and echo in the space...but still, there's no reply.

It's then that I have a terrible thought. What if the reason he's not answering is because he *can't?* Perhaps they've silenced him...or worse. Maybe they did away with him after getting the information to turn this realm into a trap for me.

I circle the courtyard, staying clear of the network on the ground. *"Will!"* I'm so wired, I'm breathing fire with each new cry, lashing the night with tongues of flame as blazing hot as the magically-juiced adrenaline surging through my arteries.

I should have been more careful. Suddenly, the ground

shakes harder, and I stumble. My latest fiery exhalation lances downward, stabbing at the grass...and the edge of the network of lines.

What happens next comes too fast to stop. The nearest line catches, and a hot spark shoots along it like a fiery molten bead. Where the line intersects other lines, the spark divides and leaps along them in parallel, sizzling toward still other strands in the network.

Sparks race up and into some of the tubes, and they burst to life, ejecting fast-moving projectiles straight into the sky. There's a shuddering *boom*, then another, and I raise my shield high, expecting shrapnel.

This must be it, the other shoe dropping. Appearances can be deceiving in the Suckyverse, and this must be the war zone on the flipside of paradise.

More of the tubes blow, and projectiles boom overhead. I grit my teeth and swing my scythe, ready to repel every threat.

"Come on, then!" I wail. "Do your worst! You won't take *me!*"

It's then that I see the sky erupt in a shower of flickering gold sparkles, followed by a blossom of red.

"What the hell?" I lower my shield a little and gape with wonder.

How many explosions and lightshows have I seen throughout the Suckyverse, all of them ominous or calamitous in some way or another? Yet how often have I seen one like *this* since leaving home? How often have I seen honest-to-God, ooh-and-ah *fireworks* since I followed Will up that ladder?

The answer is *never*.

But what if the fireworks are weaponized somehow, meant to rain down destruction on me? The answer to *that* question, and so many more, becomes very clear when the next big shell takes to the air. There's a loud *thump* as it launches, then a *whoosh* as it shimmies into the heights—and the biggest *boom* yet as it explodes.

This time, the burst of light is red and shaped like a giant heart with words burning in the center of it.

I love you, Mia.

I can't believe my eyes. It's the *message*, the one I've been *waiting for*.

"Will?"

The heart fades as another shell blazes to life in its place— more words, written across the sky in twinkling yellow letters.

I'm right here, Mia.

Again, the words fade and are replaced by another firework:

We're finally together

(And another firework after that.)

After all this time.

Just then, the ground stops rumbling. "Magic Man" plays over the speakers in the gazebo. My doubts and suspicions falter and fade like embers on the night wind.

"I don't understand." My shield comes down all the way, and I step forward, calling out to him. "Where *are* you?"

More booms, more words in the sky: *When I got here, this place was a blank.*

And a dead end.

The door that let me in
Was one-way only,
So no way out.
More booms, more words: *What to do?*
I knew you'd follow me here someday,
But I might die of old age
In the meantime.
I wanted us to be together,
But how to stay alive until then?
The words keep coming: *Finally realized*
I could JOIN with this blank place,
Become AGELESS,
And REMAKE it
Just for US.
Now, this place is...
The biggest shell yet booms like a thunderclap, and the biggest, brightest word emblazons the starry sky: *...ME!*

I look around in wonder. Lights dance in the stores of the strip mall. Deer emerge from back doors into the courtyard, joined by rabbits and squirrels. Chirping songbirds glide in and roost on the gazebo.

Meanwhile, the fireworks continue:
I waited so long.
CENTURIES?
MILLENNIA?
Now I'm so HAPPY
You're here.
I stand down, relaxing my battle stance. My scythe and shield become my arms again. I stop breathing fire, and my hair stops burning.

So this is what happened to Will? A *man* became a *place*? And the *place* became...my *home?*

How do I feel about that?

Again, he speaks through fireworks:

Can you still LOVE me?

Now that I'm a PLACE?

Now that I'm a WORLD?

I think for a moment, letting it all settle in. This isn't what I *hoped* for, is it? This isn't what I *dreamed* of.

All this time, across ten thousand realms (and more), the vision of our eventual reunion sustained me. The thought of his loving arms around me, of kisses and lovemaking *epic* in nature.

Is it enough, now, to find him so changed, so present yet so *unreachable* in the ways I've longed for? Can I accept a *life* and a *love* with so much *strange* and *missing?*

Even as I think it, I laugh to myself. *Seriously?* When was the last time my life or love was anything *but* that way?

Smiling, I spread my arms wide. "You have *always* been my world," I tell him. "My place has *always* been with you."

Fireworks flurry in the sky, red and blue and yellow and green: *I was hoping you'd say that.*

The sun rises suddenly, and the wind becomes a soft breeze. A familiar doe walks up and licks my hand. Hummingbirds circle around me, tiny wings beating and blurring.

Somehow, I feel Will all around me, his life force emanating from the sky and land and water like an element. Though no human body contains him, he is *here*, his love exuding from every animate and inanimate thing.

I will never be without him again, and *he* will never be without *me*.

Finally, at the end of the road, I've found a place I don't want to leave. It turns out there's *one* realm in all the Sucky-verse that *doesn't* suck.

KRISTINE KATHRYN RUSCH

Kristine Kathryn Rusch is a New York Times and USA Today bestselling writer and maybe the most award-winning and prolific writer working today. She has won more awards in science fiction and mystery than just about anyone alive and she is the only person to win the Hugo Award for her writing as well as her editing.

This time travel science fiction short novel will hook you right from the start. Be ready to give it time to read.

You can find out a lot more about Kris's work at her publisher, WMG Publishing Inc www.wmgbooks.com or her website www.kriswrites.com.

THE TOWER

KRISTINE KATHRYN RUSCH

H e had gotten a message.

Sent by old-fashioned tradecraft dating from the days of the Secret Intelligence Service, long before the advent of MI6. A simple flowerpot on a balcony in Kensington, a tiny red flag next to the ugliest flower Thomas had ever seen.

The flower didn't matter. The flag did.

It meant: *Be at the designated spot, midnight.* Be prepared.

So Thomas stood on London Bridge, his back to the traffic, his arms resting on the railing. To his left, the lights of Southwark Cathedral. To his right, the Monument designed by Sir Christopher Wren to remind everyone of the Great Fire of London in 1666.

Thomas pretended to contemplate the lights of London reflected on the water. A bit of a wind brushed his cheeks, bringing the slightly bitter scent of the Thames.

Behind him, cars hummed as they glided by. Someone would notice him sooner or later. A man standing on London

Bridge at midnight, his arms resting on the edge, looking down at the water, spoke of melancholy at the very least, a potential suicide at the very worst.

His hair ruffled as the breeze grew stronger.

Then he felt someone at his shoulder and he braced himself so that he couldn't be tossed over. His heart was pounding.

Paranoia, that's all it was. He was here to do a job, not to be killed.

Still, he stepped slightly to his left, just enough to take him out of harm's way.

"Lovely night." The voice was husky, unfamiliar—and surprisingly—female.

Thomas looked at her out of the corner of his eye. She was slight, hair cropped short, rounded cheeks reddened from the chill breeze. Maybe thirty, maybe younger.

"I've seen better." He spoke the coded response, half expecting her to go off script. After all, it was a lovely night, and strangers occasionally said such things to each other, even at midnight on London Bridge.

"I saw better on New Year's," she said. "The way the fireworks seemed to float through the Eye."

She *was* his contact then. Somehow he had always imagined the insider was a man. Middle-aged, disgruntled. Willing to be bought off. Thomas had been watching all of them—those that he could, anyway—wondering who would meet him when the time came.

Odd that he missed a woman. Maybe that's why he had. She seemed shadowy, inconspicuous, perfect for this kind of corporate espionage.

"These days," he said, "fireworks remind me of Guy Fawkes Day when I was a boy."

"Shame they can't blow up Parliament today." She turned toward him and grinned.

He didn't grin back, but he did check, out of the corner of his eye, to see if anyone approached. Aside from the cars humming behind them, the Bridge was empty.

"So?" he asked. "You have a date certain?"

"Two, actually," she said. "The first is Wednesday at five p.m. West Wall, White Tower. The second is July, 1674."

"1674?" he asked. "I don't want that year."

"It's your only hope," she said. "They don't like doing remotes. You're lucky. The researcher is highly regarded, but female. She doesn't dare walk across the Thames. She has to be on location."

He shook his head. "I want 1650, early September 1666, or 9 May 1671. 1674 is too late."

"You've also made your impatience known," she said. "If you want to finish your job in the next year, you'll take 1674. It's the only remote planned."

"They're not doing other remotes?" He certainly wouldn't hear of them. He did work at Portals, just like this woman did, but he had never been assigned to the technical areas. The managers had actually given tests to all applicants, and he had failed the mathematical portions. But he had aced the history sections. So he'd spent the past two years in research, finding out tiny things for major historians, and growing more and more impatient.

"They're afraid of remotes. They've only done one, and it

was controlled. This is the first uncontrolled remote, and some think it too dangerous."

"Uncontrolled?" he asked.

"Into a site where they don't know each and every detail. They don't even have the government's permission." She was staring at the Thames.

He did too, watching the lights ripple on the inky black water. He could get caught on this end, then, not by Portales, but by the British government. But there were no laws against time travel. Not yet.

"You have to be careful," she said as if reading his thoughts. "This is the first such major experiment. Try not to cock it up."

Cock it up. As if he were part of the corporate team. He didn't care if they never had another remote, so long as he got his treasure.

But he wasn't sure how he would go about it, even with this remote. "What happened in July of 1674?"

The woman didn't answer. Instead, she stared at the Thames for a moment. Then she said, "You're the fake historian. You figure it out. And, by the way, your portal is Neyla Kendrick. Good luck."

His portal. A pun. He hated puns, and was about to tell her when he realized she was walking away from him. The breeze carried her vanilla perfume long after her footsteps faded.

He had been told his contact would arrange the right time period, and make sure he could do his job with a minimum of fuss. Everything would be timed to the second.

He needed it timed. He needed it just so.

He could call it off, he supposed. His client would hire

someone else, someone with less caution, someone with a few more balls.

Not that he lacked balls. He'd carried out some of the greatest thefts in living memory.

But this one would be the pinnacle of his career—not just in money, but in audacity.

The Crown Jewels.

Not all of them of course. The most famous ones as well as the ones still in use had to remain. But the minor ones, the ones he'd researched, the ones no one had done much more than stare at under glass for hundreds of years, he could take any one of those, and would.

If he decided to do this.

1674—July.

He thought he'd covered all the possible opportunities to steal the jewels in the 17th century.

What had he missed?

_____

The thick linen tape actually put pressure on her chest. Neyla Kendrick had trouble drawing a breath.

"That's too tight," she said to McTavish, who was trying to dress her.

The Closet was cold. Rows of clothing, all on racks, all from different time periods, ran off into the distance.

She felt like she was in one of the old warehouses that used to line this part of Southwark after the Second World War. She had to remind herself that beyond the double doors was a modern well-lit hallway.

McTavish tugged at the tape one more time.

"That *hurts*," she said.

He let go and the tape unraveled. She took a deep breath for the first time since he had wrapped the stuff around her. She looked down. Red welts covered the fleshy part of her upper breasts.

"Just get the reduction," McTavish said. "You can have them inflated when you get back."

As if her breasts were balloons. She glared at him.

McTavish had been a dresser, a costumer, and finally a designer for the London Stage. Portals, Inc. had hired him away with an obscene salary, mostly for his knowledge of historical fashion. Not just because he knew how to make someone look like they were from, say, the Middle Ages, but because he could actually pinpoint a year. He could find or make materials that fit so accurately, no native of the time period would think anything was wrong.

McTavish wasn't that careful with his own clothing. He wore the standard long frock coat—this season's current design for the fashionable man—but his was velvet, and too hot. He always smelled faintly of sweat.

"I'm not going to get my breasts reduced," Neyla said. "I'm leaving Wednesday morning."

"It's cosmetic," he said. "It'll be done in less than an hour. You'll have no pain at all. And when you get back—"

"They have to put some substance inside my breasts. It won't be me any more. I like having the original equipment."

He raised his eyebrows at her. "You also want to do your research, right? With those honkers, no one's going to mistake you for a boy, not unless I wrap all of your torso."

"I won't be bathing," she said, still shuddering at the very idea. She was going back to the land of unwashed flesh, fleas, and bedbugs. That was what she feared the most. The bugs, the dirt, the way she would have to live it all.

"It'll be July," McTavish said. "Hottest month of the year in any century. You'll already be wearing more clothing than you're accustomed to. The last thing I want is for you to get heatstroke. Another reason not to bind these puppies. Get them reduced."

"No," she said. "You're going to flatten them and you're going to make it look natural."

Then she grabbed her pink cotton shirt and pulled it on, leaving her bra on the nearby rack as if she had forgotten it. She wasn't going to wear anything over "those puppies." She was going back to work.

"It's not going to look natural," he said.

"Neither are my teeth," she said, "but I'm not having those pulled for verisimilitude either."

Then she stalked out of the Closet.

She was getting angry at McTavish and that wasn't right. He was just a perfectionist, trying to make her the best 17th century male she could possibly be. He was trying to protect her.

She appreciated the attempt at protection. But she wasn't going to give up her breasts. She had given up enough for her work. Just moving to London was enough of a sacrifice.

She was a San Francisco girl, born and raised. She loved the cool air, the fog, the modern buildings and the lack of history. She had gotten all of her degrees at UC-Berkeley, as well as two post-docs, one assistant professorship, followed by a full professorship with summers off and tons of university support to go all over the world to investigate old bones.

She had been about to accept a tenured position when Portals, Inc. contacted her, asking her to submit a proposal for their top-secret project.

Time travel. Controlled, examined. Portals wanted to investigate all kinds of historical avenues before taking its product public. It was a giant form of beta testing. If something went wrong for the historians investigating old myths, virologists investigating ancient diseases, and biologists trying to get DNA from long-vanished species, then Portals would do more testing on its travel system.

Neyla's proposal was simple: It was a redraft of her undergraduate honors thesis, which she had written in conjunction with the History, English, and Anthropology departments. Her thesis was an analysis of the importance of the Princes in the Tower, as told by their bones. Not that she had seen their bones, of course. No one alive had. The bones had been examined only once, in 1933. What then passed for modern science concluded that the bones belonged to two young boys who were the right age to be the princes, and therefore probably were.

That conclusion was enough for the British government. Since then, they hadn't allowed anyone to examine the bones.

She hadn't expected Portals to care about the ancient mystery of the Princes in the Tower, but apparently they had received so many requests from historians and amateur crime buffs, all of whom wanted to solve the mystery themselves (and wanted to spend a year in 1483 and 1484 doing so), that the Portals CEO, Damien Wilder, figured this could be the signature project.

He had been looking for someone who knew how to solve the mystery of the Princes' deaths in a short visit to the past. Neyla's proposal was the shortest—a return to July of 1674, when the skeletons were discovered on the south side of the White Tower. Unfortunately, no one had a date certain, so anyone hoping to find the bodies might have to spend the entire month in 1674—which was a prospect she was now facing.

She stepped inside her office, her heart pounding. She was still angry over McTavish's comment. Not because he had any power to make her go through even minor physical changes for this project, but because he had tapped into her fears about this trip.

So many risks. She had to somehow pose as one of the workers or someone who belonged at the Tower during July of 1674. She and her team would be traveling with only the minimum of supplies, a second set of clothing, and the minia-turized scientific equipment.

She slipped behind her desk. Beyond the large glass windows, London sprawled. The skyscape looked nothing like the skyscape in 1674. Then the Tower housed some of the largest buildings in the city. Now century-old buildings dwarfed it. Even the creaky London Eye made the Tower look like a hunk of the past stuck in the middle of the present.

She pulled out the box holding the equipment she would take with her. The box was long and thin as if it contained a necklace from Tiffany's. Inside were small items designed to look like things from 1674, a quill pen, a pin, a ring. They all housed something important from her computer (complete with camera and voice recorder) to the many backups she needed.

Everything was solar powered, which helped. Her traveling companions would have redundant equipment, so if someone lost theirs, they wouldn't lose the information.

The entire trip could be summed up in this small box. If she didn't get the right information at the right time in the right way, the trip and all its dangers would be for nothing.

She couldn't quite get over her own audacity.

To travel into one of the world's most heavily guarded places, to a place still more famous for its prisoners and executions than for its grandeur and its coronations, took a degree of chutzpah she would never have guessed that she had.

Finally she stood and walked to the window. The Thames glittered in the sunlight. Cars flowed over the bridges and through the city, like blood through veins. She was too high to see people walking. From this vantage, though, she could see the entire Tower complex from Traitor's Gate up front to the Jewel House toward the back and the White Tower in the very middle.

Dark and old, foreboding and entrancing, the Tower at this moment was filled with tourists and schoolchildren, people who had paid to "experience" the past.

In two days, she would join them, pretending to be that peculiar kind of tourist who dressed up in period dress to enjoy an historical monument.

In two days, she would stand by the White Tower, and become someone else.

Neyla Kendrick was exactly the kind of person Thomas didn't want to travel with. One of those esoteric scientific types with a narrow specialty who might have to spend an entire month in the past for one moment alone with a pile of bones.

Thomas wanted to get in and get out, quick and dirty. He'd been willing to spend a few days in September of 1666, the Great Fire, just to get the right opportunity. But even his vaguer instructions for the Cromwellian era took into account the fact that the Jewels weren't very important in the Interregnum. Most got sold or lost or stolen.

Thomas had just planned to do a bit of the stealing, in a very short period of time.

Now he had to spend a month with a woman interested in the bones of children. He wasn't even sure what the fuss was about. The Princes had died hundreds of years ago, at a time when England routinely killed its monarchs. It wasn't even accurate to call the boys princes. Technically, one—Edward—was the King of England.

The son of Edward IV, Edward V's only crime was being underage and sickly. His brother Richard was the spare to the heir.

They had come to the Tower voluntarily, to prepare for Edward's reign. His uncle Richard was supposed to be the kid's Protector, the person who managed the Kingdom until the boy came of age. But something happened—historical crap no one really cared about any more—and Richard (the uncle not the spare) decided to take the Kingship for himself.

The boys lived for a while after Richard took the throne. And eventually they died—either from sickness or murder most foul. Richard became the infamous Richard the Third, known more for murdering his nephews than for his deeds as King.

Had the boys been allowed to rule, the entire history of the English monarchy might have changed.

But they hadn't been allowed to rule, and there were more than enough murders after them. Henry VIII murdered wives, for heaven's sake. His eldest daughter became known as Bloody Mary for her actions as Queen of England and his youngest daughter, Elizabeth, had been no shrinking violet.

Every English monarch of the period killed "pretenders" to the throne, some of whom had more claim to that throne than the person sitting in it.

And each death, if prevented, could have changed the course of English history.

So…two little boys? Really, who cared?

The biggest problem Thomas had wasn't with Neyla Kendrick or with the long-lost Princes. It was with his own knowledge base. He was going to replace one of Kendrick's assistants.

Thomas knew everything there was to know about the Tower during the Great Fire. He also knew everything he could possibly learn about Thomas Blood, whose attempt to steal the Crown Jewels on 9 May 1671 was one of the more famous thefts in English history.

Thomas even knew which Jewels were lost forever in the Interregnum.

He just didn't know what had joined the collection by 1674, what would be missed, and what wouldn't.

With only less than two days to find out, he didn't have time to study. This job was becoming a great deal of aggravation.

But, he had to remind himself, no amount of aggravation would make him quit.

There was no better target than this one, no better test of his skills.

To commit the crime of a lifetime took an amazing thief.

To commit the crime of several lifetimes took one of the best thieves ever.

He wanted that title for his own.

———

"He's *what?*" Neyla asked. "He's *sick?* That's not possible. Men like Peter Wilson don't get sick."

The flunky half bowed as Neyla spoke. He was scrawny, with bad teeth, and thinning hair. And he was *young*, twenty-two if he was a day. She had never seen him before, but then she hadn't seen half the people who worked for Portals before. Because he was afraid to give her bad news himself, the head of Travel had sent this poor soul to her. Apparently, the head of Travel had figured out she'd be pissed off.

"Beg pardon, ma'am," the flunky said timidly, "but Dr. Wilson's got pneumonia. He nearly died. One of his lungs collapsed. They've reinflated it and given him some kind of treatment, but he won't be well by tomorrow at five—at least not well enough to trust him alone without medical help in such a primitive time. Ma'am."

"You'd think in this day and age," she said, "no one would ever get that sick."

"Beg pardon, Ma'am," the flunky said, "but people still do get ill on occasion."

"But pneumonia? None of us should've gotten that. It's one of those things that can be prevented." She ran a hand through her hair. "This makes no sense. Pete Wilson is our biologist, our food specialist. He's the one who is supposed to prevent *us* from getting sick. He can't get sick himself, not before we go."

The flunky wisely remained silent.

"I suppose we have to call this off now." She stood, turned her back on the flunky, and went to the window. The Tower looked foreboding in the sunlight.

She half expected to feel relief, but she felt none. She wanted to go, and she wanted to go tomorrow.

"I've been told, Ma'am, that no one wants to cancel. They've assigned you someone else."

She frowned. "They've assigned...?"

She had handpicked Pete, just like she had picked the rest of her team. But her contract did give Portals the right to assign people to her team. She had argued about that, and she had lost. Portals wanted the right to send troubleshooters and others on trips to take care of potential problems.

"His name is Thomas Ayliffe," the flunky said, "and—"

"Bullshit." She turned. "They're not sending someone named Thomas Ayliffe to the Tower of London in 1674. They can't be serious."

The flunky's cheeks had turned red. "I'm not in charge—I mean, what's wrong with Thomas Ayliffe?"

"You're clearly not up on your 17th century London history," she snapped. "Who assigned this idiot to my team?"

"Mr. Wycroft, at least he's the one who told me—"

She didn't need any more. She pushed past the flunky and stormed to Wycroft's lair.

Wycroft had half of the entire twentieth floor. He had assistants everywhere. He was nominally Neyla's boss, although she really answered to Darien Wilder.

Wycroft's receptionist was an old battle-ax who had been hired away from one of Britain's stuffiest banks. She had been hired for her prim and proper attitude, and her withering looks.

But Neyla could out-wither anyone. She took one look at the battle-ax, and the woman leaned back, ceding the field. Neyla hurried past her, only to be joined by Wycroft's chief assistant, Flynn Martin.

He was short and stocky with a friendly face and dark hair just starting to go gray. People mistook him for an easy-going person, but Neyla knew better. Flynn Martin was the steel inside Wycroft's velvet glove.

"I know you're upset," Flynn said. "But, Neyla, we need this trip to go off tomorrow—"

"I'm not taking any old person along with me because you have a schedule." Neyla kept moving, past desks and fake plants and tasteful copies of sculptures from London's most famous monuments.

"We need to test the remote devices," Flynn said. "We've put a lot of planning into this—"

"So have I," Neyla said, "and I'm not going to let some idiot get in my way and blow my cover on the very first afternoon."

"Neyla, let's talk like adults—"

"Yes, let's," she said. "And since my problem is with Harrison Wycroft, I'll speak to him, not to you."

She slammed both hands against the double doors leading into Wycroft's office. The doors banged open.

Wycroft sat behind his desk, with his back to the floor-to-ceiling windows. The cityscape extended beyond him, almost as if it were a decoration in his office, the London Eye turning lazily to his right.

"Neyla," Wycroft said without saying hello, "he's the only person we have available with at least a passing knowledge of the 17th Century."

Wycroft was an obese man whose size seemed appropriate, partly because he favored three-piece black bespoke suits, bowler hats, and the ubiquitous black umbrella.

"So postpone the trip until Pete is well," Neyla said.

Wycroft sighed and waved a hand at Flynn. Flynn pulled the doors closed as he stepped back outside.

"Pete, it seems, isn't as cautious as we thought. He was dealing with bacteria from another trip, this one to the 15th century, and comparing various disease vectors, somehow infecting himself with a particularly virulent strain of Pneumocystis carinii. The problem is that he's ill and in isolation, and we're not going to get him back for weeks, maybe months. Even then he might not be cleared to travel."

She crossed her arms. "How long has he been ill?"

"He's had a cough for a week. It got worse over the weekend."

"And no one thought to warn me?"

"We hoped it wouldn't be serious."

She shook her head. She understood why Pete wasn't going. She even understood the need for haste with this trip. Portals had its various patents to protect, experiments to foster, research and development to promote. She was only one small cog in a very big wheel.

What she didn't understand was how no one seemed to understand that a man named Thomas Ayliffe would be a problem.

"This Thomas Ayliffe is pulling your chain," she said.

"What's wrong with Ayliffe?" Wycroft asked. "Have you had difficulty with him before?"

"What's wrong with him?" she snapped, stepping toward Wycroft. "What's *wrong* with him? You say he's an expert on 17th century London."

"The closest that we have on such short notice, yes," Wycroft said.

"If he's an expert," she said, "he's giving you a message. Have you done an identity check on this man?"

Wycroft slid out a drawer. He pressed something—probably one of his private networked computer links—and examined the answer.

"Yes, of course. He went through the same rather difficult vetting system that you did."

"His name is legitimate?" she asked.

"Yes." The answer came from behind her.

Neyla turned. A man stood there. He was tall, broad-shouldered, and as well dressed as Wycroft, only in a suit that wasn't half as conservative. The man had black hair, blue eyes, and ruggedly handsome features.

"I don't believe we've been introduced." His British accent was so posh that he sounded like he belonged at Buckingham Palace. "I'm Thomas Ayliffe."

"And I'm Nellie Bly," she said.

He stared at her with that same withering look that the battle-ax outside had perfected. "You can check my birth records."

"We have," Wycroft said. "Neyla, what's your objection to the man's name?"

"Apparently Ms. Kendrick believes I'm going to use the name when we go to 1674. And that would be unwise." Ayliffe walked into the room, stopping beside her. He smelled of soap, as if he had just stepped out of the shower.

She looked at him sideways. He was significantly taller than she was, which was also a problem. Brits in the 17th century, especially working class Brits, were notably short due to poor nutrition and unhealthy environmental conditions.

"You see," Ayliffe said, "Thomas Ayliffe was one of the many names used by the infamous Thomas Blood."

"Why is that a familiar name?" Wycroft asked.

"For god's sake," Neyla said. "Thomas Blood is the most famous person ever to steal the Crown Jewels."

Wycroft stared at her.

"In 1671. He failed, but spectacularly," she said. "He became a folk hero, depending on your political persuasion at the time. Remember, Cromwell was only a few years before, and not everyone believed in the restoration of the monarchy."

Wycroft raised his eyebrows.

"I can't help my family name," Ayliffe said, "but I promise not to use it when we travel. It's not like you need a passport anyway. No one checks your identification."

Neyla glared at him. He didn't even look at her. He directed all of his comments to Wycroft, which she also found irritating.

But she could do the same thing. "He's too tall," she said.

"Both Henry Tudors were over six feet," Ayliffe said.

"Henry the Seventh and his son, Henry the Eighth, were both royalty raised in the best of conditions. Besides, by 1674, they were long dead. No one would remember that they were tall. They would simply remember that Henry VIII was supremely fat."

She bit her lip, wishing she hadn't said that in front of Wycroft. She made herself continue, partly to cover her gaffe. She now turned toward Ayliffe.

"Even if they did remember how tall the Henries were," she said, "you're going to be posing as some ditch digger who probably never had real meat or fresh vegetables in his entire life. You'll stand out."

"And you won't?" He finally turned to her, then he let his gaze run up and down her entire figure.

To her own disgust, she blushed. She wasn't going to defend her appearance.

"According to his file," Wycroft said, "Mr. Ayliffe here used to participate in the Society for Creative Anachronism, so he's not averse to costuming. He works in our history department, specializing in the Elizabethan era, which isn't that much different from the era you'll be traveling in—"

"It's different enough," Neyla snapped.

"But the clothing and customs are close," Wycroft said.

"Close isn't good enough," she said. "We've been working on this for two years. We have a team."

"Pete's not going no matter how you argue it," Wycroft said. "And waiting won't help. We're just going to have to muddle through."

"Let's muddle through without the tall guy," she said. "The rest of us are ready. I don't know what he'll add."

"I do know something about food," Ayliffe said. "I spent a few years at Stratford before I realized that acting wasn't for me, so 17th century English isn't that foreign to me. I will probably be able to understand the natives better than you will."

He had a point, although she wasn't going to concede it. Everyone who studied with the Royal Shakespeare Company spent quite a bit of time learning how to speak Elizabethan English, which was still what they were speaking in the 1670s. Her American accent was going to be a handicap. She had planned to speak to the locals as little as possible.

"You will need a translator, right?" Ayliffe asked. "And I didn't see one on your list. I think that might be a lot more valuable than a biologist."

"Pete isn't just a biologist," she said. "He was in charge of food safety."

"If you want safe food, stay here," Ayliffe said. "Back there, you're going to eat things that horrify you because you have no other choice. You'll just have to trust that all those medical precautions they took here at Portals will protect you."

"Nothing will protect against food poisoning," she said.

"Expect a mild case or two," he said. "I've had it. It's not pleasant, but you'll survive."

"In the modern era," she said. "Four hundred years ago, it could kill you."

"But we'll have the remotes," he said. "We'll be able to come back if someone gets deathly ill. Right?"

He directed that last question to Wycroft.

Wycroft's mouth pursed. His eyes shifted to Neyla, then back to Ayliffe. Wycroft looked very uncomfortable.

So no one had briefed Ayliffe on all of the details. Just some of them.

Ayliffe looked from Wycroft to Neyla. "What don't I know?"

"We can return any time in the first three days," she said. "Then we have another window thirty days later. That's it."

"What do you mean, that's it?"

She shrugged. "If we miss the windows, there's a very good chance we'll get stuck back there."

She tried to sound calm about it, but she wasn't calm. She was going to monitor those windows like nothing else, and she was going to return in one of them, no matter what.

"Why?" Ayliffe asked. "You can come back any time. Time travel is time travel is time travel. It doesn't correlate. Even if you leave the past on 30 July 1674, you'll be able to arrive back here one second after you left. What's the problem?"

"It's a design flaw in the remotes," Wycroft said. "Something we haven't been able to solve yet."

"Whatever the remotes do," Neyla said, being as vague as she could be since she never really bothered to understand the science, "they work on the initial energy burst for the first three days. Then the system will go dark for a while, recharging, for lack of a better phrase. Our first opportunity to return will be in thirty days."

"Our first," Ayliffe said. "So you won't get stuck."

"We don't know that," she said. "What we do know is that only people who have used the three-day and thirty-day windows have returned. No one else has. I would assume they've tried every thirty days after that. I don't know for certain."

He frowned, then looked at Wycroft. "How do you know this? I thought this is the first major remote trip."

"You think we didn't test the remotes?" Wycroft asked. "We've been testing them for a decade."

"And you're willing to go with this design flaw?" Ayliffe sounded shocked. That pleased Neyla. Maybe he'd back out.

"It's no more dangerous than sending someone back to the 17th century," Wycroft said in that tone he used when he was spouting corporate cover-your-assisms. Neyla had heard these arguments before. In fact, she had made some of them.

"So those people who got lost," Ayliffe said, "you haven't sent teams after them?"

"Where would we look?" Wycroft asked. "And what if the problem isn't the remotes? What if they got arrested or something else happened?"

"You don't leave people behind," Ayliffe said.

"They knew the risks," Wycroft said. "So do we. There's a

chance that they wanted to stay, you know. Maybe they found true love."

He couldn't hide the sarcasm from his voice. Since Portals went public, the number of movies and novels about people finding love back in time had quadrupled.

"Most likely they died," Neyla said.

Ayliffe looked at her, obviously alarmed.

Neyla added, "If you come with us—and I think you shouldn't—you're not going to go on some sanctioned SCA field trip or some little practice holiday for Elizabethan scholars. You'll be entering a dark, dirty world more dangerous than any third world country. The longer we stay, the less chance we have of surviving."

"So let's get in and out fast," Ayliffe said.

"We can't," she said. "I don't know what day in July they discovered the bodies of the Princes. Even if I did know, I'm not sure how fast I'll be able to gain access to them."

"This is," Wycroft said, "our first experiment in a deliberately long trip. We've had accidentally long trips in the past, but not something like this."

Ayliffe visibly swallowed. He looked nervous for the first time since she had met him.

"And," Neyla said, mostly to make him more nervous, "most of those accidentally long trips happened in the time travel booth here in Portals itself. Remotes aren't the only problem with time travel."

Ayliffe studied her. Then he squared his shoulders, and looked at Wycroft.

"I suppose I have to sign waivers," Ayliffe said.

Wycroft looked relieved. For some reason, he seemed to

want Ayliffe on this trip. "You'll also have to go to medical and make certain you're both healthy enough for the trip and you have the right protections."

Ayliffe nodded, then he tipped an imaginary hat to Neyla. "Nice meeting you," he said. "Looks like we'll be spending some time together."

"Not if I can help it," she said.

———

Thomas left. He hadn't expected this much resistance. He had spent two years building his cover at Portals, making certain his identity was rock-solid and unimpeachable, and his work record perfect.

He hadn't known his allies in the company would deliberately make one of the original team ill, but it made sense. He also hadn't expected anyone to know what his name meant. But then, he had initially planned on traveling back in time alone. He had been opening the door to Wycroft's office when Neyla Kendrick had said *If he's an expert, he's giving you a message*, and he damn near turned around and left.

He'd always used names like Thomas Ayliffe on jobs. A bit of an inside joke, which meant nothing to anyone but him.

But she had seen through it—and accurately. He had sent a small message, one that he hadn't expected to be received until after he left, if he had accomplished his task.

She made him nervous.

She was also too pretty to masquerade as a boy. Too pretty and too buxom. He had no idea how the costumers were going to hide those curves, but they had quite a job ahead of them.

Which reminded him. He needed clothes for the journey.

He had a lot to do before five o'clock tomorrow. He hoped he could finish everything in time.

————————

At four o'clock on Wednesday, the team assembled in Neyla's office, dressed in appropriate clothing, all in varying shades of brown. Some of the brown had nothing to do with dye. McTavish had dragged white shirts through mud and dirt and let them dry, then tried to wash them by hand with lye soap. The shirts weren't so much brown as a kind of crap-colored dark tan.

Neyla's breasts had finally been tamed, and the wrapping didn't even hurt. McTavish, working with some of the scientists, found a nice mixture of spandex and nanotechnology to squish her breasts. Then McTavish wound some regular cloth around her belly, so that she looked like a man who had a barrel chest, rather than a pretty boy with man-boobs.

When she looked at herself in the mirror, with her short hair, barrel chest, and spindly legs, she seemed like something out of Hogarth—one of the wide-eyed commoners crowding around the subject of the drawing on crammed streets of London.

The rest of her team looked authentic too—at least to her. Jeff Renolet, who didn't need wrapping to create his own barrel chest, stood beside her. He was in his forties, balding, with a ruddy face. He normally wore crowns on his front teeth, but Portals' dentist had removed them for this trip. Jeff looked like an old fat man who had been repeatedly punched in the mouth.

Next to Jeff, Benedict Ivance scratched underneath one arm. He had chosen loose-weave linen, which held dirt in every single wrinkle. Modern linen had been treated so that it was soft, but linen without treatment was rough. If he was scratching already, he would be raw by the time this trip was over.

Compared to the others, Dan Sheldon looked like a half-grown boy. He was whip-thin thanks to his daily six-mile runs and his love of urban free climbing. His eyes were clear, his blond hair cut in a bowl-shape. He had the kind of inno-cent face that often showed up in religious paintings of the era. Instead of his filthy clothes, he should have been wearing priest's robes.

Thomas Ayliffe towered over all of them. His clothing was a bit upscale for a member of the working class, but McTavish had taken care of that by ripping it, mending it, and then ripping it again. Ayliffe looked like an elegant man who had come upon hard times.

Besides, Neyla was beginning to think the man would look good in anything.

She hated that she found him attractive. He was annoying and in the way, and he was noticeable. He was going to scotch this mission just by being part of it. She knew it, and she resented it.

She had done everything she could to get rid of him. She had spent fifteen minutes after Ayliffe left Wycroft's office, trying to convince him to take Ayliffe off the team. When that didn't work, she had gone all the way to Damien Wilder's office, only to be told that Wilder was in Japan, making some kind of presentation.

She was stuck with elegant, good-looking Ayliffe and with his ripped upscale clothes.

Her party's cover story was simple. They had joined up on a trip to London to find work. They'd been in the city only a few months and had found just enough to keep them alive.

Theoretically, the story explained their extra clothing, their bundles of supplies and the fact that none of them looked like the other. Friends and colleagues, not relatives.

They'd had the story drummed into them, practicing it and everything else at odd moments. Neyla, the only one without a British accent, had vowed not to speak much, at least around natives. But the others had to be careful as well. Jeff had studied 17th century speech and Ayliffe knew Elizabethan English, but neither of them had heard it spoken correctly.

They double-checked their equipment one last time. Everyone had their own remote, as well as their own tiny computers. Some had specialized equipment. Ayliffe got custody of Pete's food safety devices, with a short instruction on how to use them. Because Pete wasn't coming along, Neyla insisted on double the amount of water purification tablets even if that meant a little extra bulk in their kits.

When they were done, she looked at the entire group.

"Last chance to back out," she said.

They stared at her. Jeff's right eye had developed a nervous tick. Benedict bit his lower lip, as if he were trying not to say anything, and Dan took a deep breath, clearly trying to calm himself.

Only Ayliffe looked like a man about to go on an adventure. His eyes were bright, his cheeks slightly flushed.

"All right, then," she said. "Off we go."

———

They took a cab to the western entrance, and piled out like the excited tourists they were pretending to be. Neyla gazed up at the massive stone entrance, as impressive now as it had been the first time she had come here. Her stomach did a slight flip, and her breath caught.

Now it all felt real to her.

She followed her little troop through the arches, past the buskers and the tradesmen offering everything from a printout of that day's news to Tower trinkets supposedly for less than they were being sold for inside.

Almost no one walked in with her group. What tourists they saw were leaving. The Tower closed to visitors at six, and most people had spent all day here.

The modern gift shop looked garish in front of the Middle Tower. Neyla walked past it to the matching ticket booths. They seemed as out of place as the gift shop, but at least they didn't block the old entrance to one of the towers.

She hurried up to the window, the other members of her team following her.

"Five tickets," she said, broadening her American accent and filling her voice with excitement.

The ticket taker, an elderly woman with a kind face,

leaned toward the plastic separating her from Neyla. "Ah, luv, I've got to charge you full price, and you'll only get an hour in there. Come back tomorrow noon latest, and you'll be able to enjoy the whole place."

"I'm flying home tomorrow," Neyla lied, sounding as disappointed as she could.

The ticket taker sighed, as if this were her problem, not Neyla's. "Then you're better off, luv, walking the outside for free, taking pictures and looking at the ravens. It's a lot of money for just an hour, and I don't feel right selling you a ticket."

Just sell me a damn ticket, Neyla wanted to snap. *I'm sure your bosses would appreciate the revenue.*

But she smiled instead. "You're so kind. But my friends here want to see the Crown Jewels, and I want to see where Anne Boleyn got her head cut off."

The ticket taker winced at Neyla's crudeness, but it worked. Playing the demanding American got her exactly what she wanted.

She bought five tickets, then led her little group back to the Middle Tower. The Middle Tower had been an entrance into the entire complex since the beginning of the 14th century. It had to have been impressive then, so tall and formidable and new.

Neyla knew the history of each and every building. She knew who built it and why, its various uses, and when it was remodeled, moved, or, in a few cases, destroyed. She carried multiple maps of the entire complex in her head, just in case the remotes worked improperly. The last thing she wanted was to overshoot their historical timeslot and end up inside the wall of a building that had later been torn down—or a moat that had been filled in.

Her group had quite a trek from the Middle Tower down Lanthorn Lane to the Bloody Tower, which would take them to the Inner Ward. Tourists had gone on a prescribed walk ever since the Tower was opened to the public, centuries ago.

She knew there were other ways inside the Tower's defenses, she just wasn't allowed to take those ways as a member of the public.

As her team walked, they gawked at their surroundings like proper tourists. The real tourists gawked at them, dressed in their period costume. They received several stares and more than a few people pointed at them.

Neyla tried to ignore them all. She kept her eye on the Bloody Tower, as she had since the first time she had come here. It got its name from the Princes. The Bloody Tower was the last place they'd been seen alive, looking out the windows in 1483. Over time, no one saw them any more, and Tudor historians claimed Richard III had murdered them there.

Of course, no one knew exactly what happened to the Princes, if indeed they were murdered there or anywhere else. Even if they had died there and the 1933 examination of the bodies was correct, then someone had taken the corpses and carried them across the grounds to the Innermost Ward, where they were buried in the foundation of a spiral staircase.

The bodies had been found in 1674, when workers getting rid of a forebuilding attached to the White Tower dug into the foundation of that staircase. The workers hadn't been surprised.

It wasn't unusual for bodies to be buried all over the

Tower's grounds. After all, the place had served as a prison from its very beginnings over 1,000 years ago. Many times, unidentified skeletons were discovered throughout the complex; more than once, dozens of bodies were discovered at the same time.

Generally no one cared who the skeletons belonged to. The Princes were one of the few exceptions.

The team reached the Bloody Tower, but didn't stop. Neyla didn't look at the windows like she usually did and wonder which ones had provided Edward V's last view of the world.

Now the team had entered the Inner Ward, where the Tower's most famous history occurred. Here, on these grounds, Henry VIII had conducted the beheadings of his rivals and wives. Here Elizabeth the First, when she was imprisoned in the Bell Tower by her sister Mary, walked every day with an escort, probably trying not to look at the spot where her mother had died.

"We're nuts," Jeff whispered.

"You want to back out?" she asked him, feeling a surge of disappointment.

He shook his head slowly, as if he were warring with himself. "Just didn't expect it to feel so real, you know?"

She did know. They stopped on the west side of the White Tower, the oldest building in the entire complex. William the Conqueror had built it in 1097 out of gleaming white Caen stone. It had stood alone on the banks of the Thames, a large Norman keep, the tallest building in all of England, twenty-seven meters high.

Neyla looked up all those meters. The Caen stone had held

up well. It no longer gleamed, but it still looked white, partly because of the cleanings that it routinely suffered now that preservationists had decided that the filth in the air would eventually cause the stone to decay.

One of the Yeoman Warders, in his regulation Elizabethan black and red garb (tourists called the Warders Beefeaters, which made her think of gin), approached their group. He turned to Ayliffe, as if Ayliffe were their leader.

"You only have about a half hour, lad, if you're going to see anything important. We shut down promptly at six."

"Thanks," Ayliffe said. "We're nearly done."

The Warder nodded, then wandered away, probably to give his warning to the other remaining tourists.

"We'd better act fast," Dan said.

"We're going to take our time," Neyla said. Going too fast might cause mistakes. The first—and most important—thing they had to do was find the right spot on the ground outside the White Tower.

The grass had been cordoned off—too many feet would cause the stuff to stop growing—but the grass not too far from the northwest corner of the White Tower was exactly where they wanted to stand. They couldn't get anywhere near that demolished forebuilding, since no one knew exactly how big it had been.

Benedict watched the Warders. He would give the team the all clear when they could run for the grass. The rest of the team pulled out their remotes.

The remotes were thin disks that looked like badly crafted circles that hung from a chain. Only right now, no one in the group wore theirs. They were instead squeezing the disk's sides to turn it on.

The technical team already programmed the date and time in. No one on Neyla's team knew how to program these things, even though she begged for the chance to learn back when this trip got scheduled.

She wanted to control when she returned. But she was told that the remotes were so delicate that one mistake could send her into a different time period, and strand her there forever.

She wasn't sure she believed it. Portals was a corporation after all, and divisions in corporations did their very best to hoard knowledge so that they could hoard power. But she hadn't won this argument either.

When she finished turning her device on, she took Benedict's and started it. Then she and the team waited while he watched.

Finally, he nodded. The group hurried to their spot on the grass, and when Neyla gave the signal, pressed the center of the disks, activating the travel mechanism.

She clutched her disk so hard, she was afraid she was going to break it. At first, nothing happened. She glanced over at the Bloody Tower, saw a Warder running toward them, and then he simply faded away.

Everything went completely black. A wind buffeted her, changing direction constantly. Thunder clapped—or maybe she was hearing sonic booms—and the air grew hotter, then colder, then hotter again.

For a moment, she felt like she was falling, and then she

realized she really was falling. She landed in a heap on the hard ground, the wind gone, the air warm and fetid.

She blinked hard, realized the darkness wasn't quite absolute. A moon shone above her and the stars surrounded it.

She'd never been able to see the stars in London before.

"Anyone else here?" she asked quietly.

She sat up, stretched her limbs, and realized that while she didn't have any broken bones, she would be badly bruised.

Her heart was pounding.

"I'm here," Dan said, his voice as soft as hers. "Hit my head pretty hard."

Her eyes were adjusting. She could see the outlines of the White Tower now, and thought she might see a dim light through one of the windows. A dim, flickering light. A lantern, perhaps, or a candle.

"You all right?" she asked.

"I think so," he said.

She moved toward his voice. She craved real light—a flashlight, a small phone/computer display, something. She hadn't planned on the darkness.

It felt like a live thing. A close, smelly live thing. Her eyes burned. The air was filled with smoke.

She hadn't expected that either.

"Anyone else here?" she asked as she groped for Dan. Finally her hand found wool.

"Ouch," he said and pulled away. "I banged myself something awful."

"Me, too," she said.

"God. They said we'd fall. They didn't say it would be so far." That voice belonged to Benedict. "You'd think they could calculate how much dirt and fill and stuff accumulated over the centuries."

Neyla sighed in relief at hearing his voice.

"Are you all right?" she asked Benedict.

"Banged up, just like Dan, but nothing serious."

"They said we'd fall only a few decimeters. Did that seem like a few decimeters to anyone? Seemed like at least a meter to me," Dan said.

Neyla had no idea. The fall was expected but hard. She was beginning to worry that Jeff and Ayliffe were too badly injured to speak.

"Experts don't know everything." That was Jeff. He half mumbled it. "I don't think they considered the tiny details. After all, they weren't the ones traveling in time."

Neyla was relieved to hear his voice. "Any broken bones, Jeff?"

"Twisted my ankle, but I can put weight on it. I'll be all right."

All the voices were close to her. She let out a sigh. "What about you, Thomas? You okay?"

Silence. She heard her own breath, a little ragged as it went in and out. Beside her, fabric rustled. Then someone's joint made a cracking noise.

"Thomas?" Why would Ayliffe pretend to be hurt? Why wouldn't he answer? "Feel around for him, guys. Maybe he got knocked unconscious."

She kept her voice down as she spoke. She didn't know if guards patrolled the grounds.

Clearly, her team had arrived at night. Which was good on one level—she would be able to see how far the work progressed, maybe even find the bodies herself—and bad on another. She would have to figure out what to do with her team before dawn, whether or not they would leave the complex or find a place to sleep somewhere nearby, somewhere that they wouldn't get caught.

"I'm not finding him," Jeff said.

"Me, either," Benedict said.

"Hey, Thomas!" Dan raised his voice slightly.

Neyla's eyes were adjusting to the darkness. She made out the shapes around her. The three men, Benedict slightly prone, Dan sitting up, and Jeff, on his hands and knees groping for Ayliffe. The White Tower in front of her. An amazing expanse of ground behind her.

The Grand Storehouse hadn't been built yet nor converted to the Waterloo Barracks. She could see what had been, in Henry III's time, the outer wall, extending all around her. As she turned, she thought she saw movement.

She squinted.

Someone was running silently across the grounds.

Away from her.

"Crap," she said and stood up. "Is that Thomas?"

She pointed toward the shadowy figure.

"It's got to be a guard," Dan said, sounding slightly panicked.

"He's not running toward us," Jeff said.

"Maybe he's getting help," Benedict said.

"No, he's not." Neyla stood and wobbled just a little. Her muscles felt like they'd been stretched and turned inside out. "It's Thomas."

"Why would he run?" Jeff asked.

"He's probably disoriented," Dan said.

"He's not that either," she said.

She should have trusted her instincts.

Thomas Ayliffe aka Thomas Blood.

The damned idiot *had* been sending a message.

And she was finally, *finally* receiving it.

———

R unning proved harder than he thought. Thomas had fallen hard on his tailbone, knocking the wind out of him. He had lain for a moment on the cool grass.

He had expected the air to stink, but not something this foul. It was as if he had landed inside a dumpster filled with raw meat on a hot summer evening.

While he tried to catch his breath, he willed his eyes to adjust to the darkness.

The darkness was great luck. He could get to Martin Tower, where the Jewels were kept in the 17th century, with a minimum of fuss, so long as he stayed away from any guards. Then he could take the Jewels, come back somewhere near here, and press his damn remote, all within his three day window.

Hell, if he did it fast enough, he would be inside a three-hour window.

Provided he could stand.

The fall had hurt. He had probably landed on some of the things he'd squirreled inside his linen shirt. He'd brought a paste copy of one of the rings he wanted, as well as some keys and a few small weapons. Tools of the trade, which had probably added to his bruises.

Neyla's voice, sounding musical, American and out of place, asked if everyone was all right. Thomas got onto his hands and knees, stifling a moan as he bent his back.

He crawled along the grass, his fingers finding mud—or something worse. He didn't want to look up. He had no idea how the sewer system worked in the Tower. Did people have privies here? Where did they dump the chamber pots?

He shuddered so deeply that he almost moaned again, but the thought was enough to get him to his feet.

Once on his feet, he could see the outline of the wall built in 13th century. Martin Tower stood on the upper northeast corner, and he could see it vaguely.

He felt disoriented. Knowing that buildings wouldn't be here—the museum for one, the Jewel House for another, Waterloo Barracks for a third—wasn't the same as seeing the grounds without them.

It looked like a completely different place.

It was a completely different place.

He brushed his hands on his knee breeches, grabbed his small bundle of supplies, and started to run as silently as he could.

He headed up the path toward the Martin Tower, ignoring the pain that ran up his spine. His whole body hurt, but he was trying to convince himself that it was the kind of hurt a man got when he had the wind knocked out of him, not when he was seriously injured.

He had to remember the plan.

There would be guards. He had read somewhere, in one of the contemporaneous accounts, that the guards around the Jewels had doubled after Thomas Blood's failed attempt in 1671.

Which was just three years ago now.

Weird.

He had to take out the guards. Break into the Jewel cupboard, and take his items.

If he was really lucky, he would get away completely. Neyla would think he somehow never made it to 1674, and she would go on with her mission without him.

He would complete his theft and be on his way.

With things more precious than gold.

———

N eyla was running before she even realized what she was doing.

She wasn't going to let that arrogant bastard ruin her trip.

She heard one of the men behind her call her name and another shush him. Then she heard footsteps, also from behind her, and hoped it was her team running with her.

She sprinted after Ayliffe. He had too much of a lead for her to catch him, but that didn't matter. Once he reached Martin Tower, he wouldn't be able to get in.

It was locked, and the guards had been doubled in the past three years. He probably didn't know that.

Her breath was coming in small gasps. Her throat tickled. The foul air made her want to cough.

So far, no guards, but that would change. Didn't they hear the commotion in the yard? Weren't they trained to come running?

But she hadn't been able to find out how many guards were on duty in July 1674. Even if she had, it wouldn't have mattered. Corruption was so deep in the Tower that just because someone was supposed to work, it didn't mean that he actually showed up.

She couldn't see Ayliffe any longer. He had to have reached Martin Tower.

Her breath came hard and suddenly she couldn't catch it at all. She wheezed and doubled over, coughing so hard that it hurt. Something was getting to her.

Lack of oxygen. The odors. The smoke.

Something.

Her eyes watered, but she made herself stagger forward.

She had to catch him, before he doomed them all.

———

M ain doors were locked, just like he expected. The locks were built into the iron doorframe, just like the old diagrams had shown.

He made himself take deep breaths of the thick air. He needed to slow down his heart rate and remain calm.

Then he reached inside his jacket, lifted the edges of his linen shirt, and felt until he found the two tools he would need right now.

The skeleton key, which he had been told was universal,

and a teeny tiny stun gun, one that didn't shoot its barbs over a distance. Instead, its business end sent an up-close-and-personal charge through the victims that they wouldn't soon forget.

His hands were shaking. He willed himself to settle down.

He could hear footsteps along the path, then wheezing and loud coughing. He couldn't tell if the cougher was male or female.

Someone wasn't taking well to the 17th century air.

He gripped the skeleton key tightly in his right hand, willed himself to do this right, and stepped in front of the door.

Then he shoved the key into the lock, and turned.

For a moment, he thought it wasn't going to work.

Then he heard an audible click.

"There is a God," he whispered. Or at least, a spirit of some kind, watching over him, helping him succeed.

———

Neyla heard a door creak open. How could the guards be missing this?

What if they weren't?

Dan and Jeff had joined her. She looked over her shoulder. Benedict was only a few yards behind them. He appeared to be running backwards, keeping an eye out behind them to protect them from potential trouble.

She reached the exterior of Martin Tower just as the door creaked closed. Something clicked.

She grabbed the handle and pulled. The door was shut tight.

Locked.

The bastard had shut them out.

Dan caught up to her. He was breathing as hard as she had been.

He tugged on the door, just like she had, and he couldn't get it open either.

"Now what the hell do we do?" she asked.

He grinned at her, then he looked at the windows on the second story.

"We climb," he said.

A lantern burned low just inside the door. A guard, sitting on a wooden chair, snapped awake as Thomas turned the skeleton key in the lock.

Thomas started. The guard was wearing the red-and-black Beefeater uniform. Only his was dirty and rumpled.

Thomas made himself take a deep, calming breath. Of course the man wore a Beefeater's uniform. The uniform had been designed in the Tudor era.

The guard spoke. For a moment, it sounded like gibberish. Then Thomas concentrated, like he used to do at the beginning of any Shakespeare play, and the words filtered through his brain.

The man had cursed. His accent was thicker than Thomas had expected, the emphasis on different parts of the words than Thomas had learned.

But they were familiar enough.

The guard stood. He was half a foot shorter than Thomas, and had gone to fat.

He smelled of grease and onions and unwashed flesh.

Thomas's eyes watered. He wondered if he would ever get used to the stinks around here.

"March away," the guard snapped. "Your place is not here."

"Oh, I belong here," Thomas said and pressed his stun gun against the guard's side.

The man burbled, then convulsed, falling backwards to the ground, his head hitting the stone floor repeatedly, sounding like some kind of drum.

Thomas watched for just a moment, making sure the man wasn't having some kind of seizure. The last thing Thomas wanted to do was kill someone.

The guard's face was red, but he seemed okay. He moaned and stopped convulsing. But he wasn't getting up.

He was breathing, though.

Thomas couldn't wait any longer. He grabbed the lantern off its peg, and hurried down the corridor to the left, hoping against hope that the Jewels were where they were supposed to be.

————

Neyla was still having trouble catching her breath. She looked up. She had free climbed in her training for this mission—part of time travel was getting in the best physical shape possible. But the free climbing she had done had been on fake rock walls in gyms, not on the side of an old stone building.

Benedict caught up to them. "We going in?"

"I am." Dan took a few more steps back, and surveyed the side of the building. "I should be able to let you in shortly after I get inside."

"If you don't get caught," Benedict said.

"O, ye of little faith," Dan said. He gripped the side of the building, then found footholds. "This thing isn't smooth. It shouldn't take me long."

Neyla was glad he didn't ask her to come along. He had asked her to urban free climb back when they were training. She had taken one look at the building that he had chosen in Canary Wharf and immediately declined to go any farther. She realized that afternoon that she had a very mild fear of heights.

He scaled the side of the building like Spider-man dressed for a Shakespeare play and reached the window in no time at all.

Neyla hadn't even realized she was holding her breath.

He braced himself, then reached into his jacket and removed the knife he had brought with him.

For a moment, Neyla thought he was going to pry the window open. Instead, he used the hilt to smash the glass.

Shards rained down on them. Jeff cursed. Benedict bent over.

Neyla was standing far enough away that she didn't get hit.

"You could've warned us," Jeff said.

She shushed him. They were already making too much noise. She turned and looked at the Inner Ward.

She wasn't sure what she was expecting—exterior security lights to go on? If someone lit a candle a few buildings away, she wouldn't be able to see it.

She turned back toward the building. Dan had disappeared inside.

Now all they had to do was wait.

———

The corridors were narrow and windy, and they smelled of tallow. Thomas kept the lantern in front of him, but it didn't give off much light. Inside the lantern's glass, four candles were carefully braced, but only one had been lit.

The stairs appeared so swiftly that he almost tripped down the first. The stone walls saved him. The walls around the stairs were so narrow that they caught him even as he pitched slightly forward.

His breathing was ragged. He put one hand on the stone wall, wincing at the stone's dampness, and went down.

He would only get one shot at this, especially now that Neyla knew he had no reason to participate in their little bone expedition.

He was glad he wouldn't have to stay here long. He hadn't expected the past to be so creepy.

He followed the twisting staircase down and relaxed slightly when he saw that it opened into a large arched room.

The cupboard was in just such a room—he'd seen someone's portrait of that. He hoped that the ancient art was accurate.

Funny, he had thought it would be easier to break into the Tower without the high level security, the cameras, the motion sensors, the laser traps.

But he had never been so terrified on a job in his entire life.

He walked forward into the darkness, holding the lantern in front of him, and wishing it gave off more light.

———

Neyla shifted back and forth on her feet. She had shushed Jeff and Benedict more than once, and then they had stopped talking altogether when a man appeared on the west side of the White Tower, slowly walking the Inner Ward.

He held a torch in one hand, but he didn't appear to be looking for anything. It took Neyla a few minutes to realize what he was doing.

He was patrolling the grounds.

She pressed what remained of her little team against the door, and pointed. They nodded. They huddled together as the man walked within a few yards of them, not noticing the broken glass or the three people a stone's throw away.

She hoped he would be gone by the time Dan got the door open.

If Dan got the door open.

She didn't know what would happen if he didn't.

———

The air down here smelled rank, almost as if the polluted Thames had flowed inside once and no one had bothered to clean it out. The walls and the floor looked clean enough—or clear enough, anyway, since there wasn't any furniture around him.

Thomas held up the lantern, hoping he wasn't hopelessly lost. Then something glinted in front of him.

His breath caught.

He was here.

Finally.

———

The guard and his torch disappeared around the front of the White Tower. Neyla let out a sigh of relief. She stepped away from the door just as something clanged inside.

Then the door creaked open and a thin ray of light trickled out.

"Come on." Dan's shadowy head peered around the door.

Jeff slid in first, followed by Benedict. Neyla entered last, pulling the heavy door closed behind her.

They were in a small antechamber of some kind. Dan had found an old-fashioned lantern, made of iron and glass, designed to protect candles from gusts of wind. The smoke from the candle wisped out of the top, near the metal ring that Dan was holding.

He nodded toward the center of the room. A guard lay flat on his back, his eyes partly open.

"Is he dead?" Jeff asked.

"Dunno," Dan said. "Thought I'd let you in first."

Neyla clenched her fist, then made herself release it, finger by finger. Dammit, dammit, dammit.

Benedict hurried over to the guard and felt his carotid artery for a pulse. After a moment, he said, "He's all right."

That was some consolation, at least. But now, no matter what, they would have to leave. They couldn't show up on the grounds the day a guard was attacked in Martin Tower.

The last thing she wanted was to get caught. Not here. In the 17th century, prisons were foul places, filled with wretched people, particularly the people who weren't wealthy and couldn't pay for their own upkeep.

"What did Thomas do to him?" Jeff asked Benedict.

"Can't tell," he said. "Doesn't look like he was stabbed. Probably hit him over the head."

"Doesn't matter," Neyla said. "We have to find Thomas and get the hell out of here."

"Out of Martin Tower?" Dan asked.

"Out of 1674," she said. "You want to be arrested here?"

"Jesus," he said. "No."

"Where are the Jewels?" Benedict asked.

She had to stop and think. She never studied much about Martin Tower. She knew the history, of course. The Jewels were locked in a ground floor cupboard, beneath the apartments of the Deputy Keeper of the Jewel House.

She had seen drawings of Blood's incredible heist, the one he had nearly gotten away with, and they always portrayed the cupboard as a large space, somewhere nearby.

But to get there directly? She had no idea.

"Was there an apartment upstairs?" she asked Dan.

"There were doors," he said. "I came in a corridor. The lantern was hanging near them. I had to use one of my matches to light it. I hope that's okay."

She didn't care that he had brought illegal matches or that he had lit the lantern. But the fact that it hung near a door not too far from the window meant that the apartments were on the west side of the building.

"We go this way," she said and headed to her left.

———————

T he light had reflected off a metal padlock someone had hung through the handles of a cupboard. The only cupboard that Thomas knew about was the Jewel cupboard.

This had to be it.

His heart was pounding so hard that for a moment, he thought someone was coming after him.

He made himself take a deep breath. He would worry about that if it happened. Right now, he needed some jewelry.

He studied the cupboard. The handles, locked shut with the padlock. But the cupboard doors themselves were hinged.

He hadn't brought a metal file, but he did have a few other tools. He could get the tiny nails out of the hinges and pull them off the door. Then the door would open from the side.

It wouldn't take long at all.

He looked around for a place to hang the lantern, found one not two feet away. He stopped, set down his bundle, then removed the candle and used it to light the other three. He replaced them and hung the lantern.

He stepped toward the cupboard and reached for the closest hinge. His hands were shaking.

He had never been so nervous on a job.

He had never done a job as complicated as this.

Thomas forced himself to relax, and slowly, carefully, pried the tiny handcrafted nails out of their hinge.

———————

They had gone through a very twisty corridor that seemed to go nowhere.

Neyla was beginning to doubt herself. She usually double-checked things in her research materials or with her computer, but she didn't have fingertip access any more.

She missed it.

She would have missed the stairs too, except that the corridor led right to them. The branch to the right, going away from the stairs, almost seemed like an afterthought.

Dan started going down the branch, but she grabbed his arm and shook her head.

Her memory said the Jewels were on the ground floor, but she wasn't sure how they defined ground floor here. Had her team come in on the ground floor or was there one level down, accessible from another part of the building?

It made more sense for the Jewel cupboard to be as far beneath ground as possible. That way it would be easier to defend.

She started down the stairs.

"I don't think so," Dan whispered. "I think they're on this floor."

"You take Benedict and look," she said. "But first, give us each a candle."

"They're not in holders," he said. "The wax'll burn your fingers."

"I don't care," she said. "I don't see well in the dark."

They stopped. He fumbled with the lantern, handing her a candle and handing Jeff one. Then he closed the glass door and picked up the lantern.

Benedict watched the whole thing as if it were a waste of time.

"If you don't find anything," Neyla said, "come back here. We'll be waiting."

At least, she hoped they would be waiting. She wasn't sure what they would find below. If they did find Thomas, she was going to have to find a way to subdue him. After all, he had almost murdered someone.

She and Jeff went down the stairs slowly.

The stone walls along the side were narrow, cramping her. The walls were damp and the air had a mildewy odor that mixed with the ripeness of stagnant water.

She resisted the urge to sneeze. Something in this time period really bothered her. She hadn't realized she had allergies until she came here.

Still, she made herself move down the stairs as quietly as she could.

When she reached the bottom she saw a series of arches that she recognized from the old paintings.

She was on the right path. She wished she could yell for Dan and Benedict, but she didn't dare.

Instead, she put a finger to her lips. Jeff nodded. Together they walked through the arches, going slowly, hoping against hope that Thomas wasn't planning to ambush them.

———

The wood was groaning, the metal scraping. Who knew 17th century craftsmanship was so damn good.

Thomas took out his knife and started digging into the wood itself. Screw the nails. The wood was the softest part of this damn cupboard. And he was going to get in no matter what.

He was making a god-awful noise. He hoped no one heard it from the apartments above. He knew from the Thomas Blood stories that one of the men in charge of the Jewels—the Keeper of the Jewel House? His deputy?—housed his entire family in Martin Tower.

It had been that family that caught Thomas Blood. The son had inopportunely returned from his military service after years away, and caught Thomas Blood's gang in the act of theft. The gang managed to escape, but the son raised an alarm and the guards caught Blood's gang in the streets just outside the Tower.

Thomas had vowed to himself that he wouldn't get caught.

So far, he seemed to be doing well.

Even if he had to gouge the damn hinges free.

———

Pounding, cursing, clanging.

Neyla glanced at Jeff, then pointed toward the sound. Two arches away, she could see a soft yellow glow.

Jeff nodded. Then he reached up and pinched his candle out.

Neyla did the same.

They pressed against each other, walking toward the noise.

It had to be Thomas.

She hoped.

———

Finally, he got the damn thing open. He pulled away an entire door, leaving it hanging from the padlock.

To his surprise, the Jewels weren't sitting on rests or in small holders. They were crammed haphazardly on shelves, looking like nothing more than some very wealthy person's high-end jewelry closet.

He stared for a moment.

He'd seen such riches before. After all, he had seen the Crown Jewels—these Crown Jewels—in their modern display, under reinforced glass with sensors all around, cameras on each jewel, special lighting, and an appropriate setting for each, showing off its sparkling magnificence.

There was no sparkling here, not even when the light caught the diamonds and sapphires and rubies. These things hadn't been cleaned in a generation.

The orb sat to one side. St. Edward's crown, restored after

Thomas Blood had crushed it to get it out of the Tower, sat near the back. Thomas couldn't see the Scepter, not that it mattered.

But he didn't want them. He wanted Edward the Confessor's sapphire ring.

He had an exquisite paste copy tied under his shirt. Or at least, what he and the forger thought was a copy. No one knew exactly what the sapphire ring looked like. It had been melted down, the sapphire placed in the Imperial Crown in 1837 for the coronation of Queen Victoria.

All they had to go on were paintings from the National Portrait Gallery and some of those lacked so much in detail that he had been praying he had it right.

Now he realized it didn't matter. The ring was probably as filthy as the rest of the jewelry, and no one knew if there was filigree work or any engravings or anything that made the ring unique.

He should have thought of that. People didn't clean *themselves* in this century. Why would they clean their jewelry?

He went through the cupboard as quickly as he could, searching for the ring.

Each time he found a small piece he could pocket, he moved it to one side. He would take a lot of lesser jewels out of here, things thought sold off to fund wars or lost to the sands of time.

Maybe lost to a traveler in time.

He grinned to himself.

Then he found Edward the Confessor's ring. Thick and well made and surprisingly heavy.

Thomas reached into his own shirt and untied the fake ring. It gleamed compared to the actual treasures.

He tied the real ring inside his shirt, put the fake with the Scepter, and then he looked at the others, trying to figure out how to carry them. He had found five pieces small enough to carry without causing too much trouble.

Counting the ring—which his sponsor saw as the real prize—Thomas would have six pieces. Five for his sponsor (in exchange for Thomas's fee) and one for himself, a keepsake of an extraordinary moment.

But he wasn't done yet.

He would put the other five pieces inside the bundle. He crouched, untied it, and spread it on the floor.

Something rustled near him. A rat? A guard?

He looked up—

And saw Neyla.

————

He had jewels. He had come to steal the Jewels, and smart bastard that he was, he took five smaller, lesser-known pieces.

Her gaze met his. He smiled.

"I figure no one will miss these," he said.

"They'd miss the guard," she said.

He raised his eyebrows. "I just stunned him."

"Lucky for you he's not dead," she said.

"I don't think that's lucky. He can identify me. I'm finishing up and getting out of here."

Her mouth opened, then closed, then opened again. Didn't he understand the implications of all of this? Didn't he realize that he had just ruined her trip? That he might get them all killed? Or maybe worse—imprisoned here, in the 17th century?

She shook with fury. "Put those things back."

He smiled again. "And do all this for nothing?"

She launched herself at him.

He tried to duck, but he couldn't, since she had already found him in a half crouch.

She hit him like a linebacker, and knocked him on his already injured tailbone. Pain swept through him, harsh and unrelenting. He couldn't catch his breath.

She grabbed him by the jaw, fingers behind his ears, and slammed his head against the hard stone floor. Once. Twice. Three times.

He twisted, pain searing through him from his back, then his head, then his back. He wrapped his hands around her wrists and tried to pull her off.

He should buck, but he couldn't get his legs underneath him. They were bent at an angle and he couldn't get purchase.

She was going to kill him. This attractive, monomaniacal bone researcher was so mad she was going to slam him to death.

He tried to gasp out an apology, but he couldn't think clearly enough to put the words together.

He wasn't sure how to stop her.

He wasn't sure if he could.

———

Hands gripped her shoulders, pulling her off.

"You're going to kill him."

Jeff had yanked her back. He was holding her.

Sweat ran down her face. She was coughing slightly. She had been gripping Thomas's jaw, her fingers digging so hard into his skin that her hands hurt.

Thomas was still on the ground, looking dazed.

If she said she hadn't meant to hurt him, she'd be lying. She had never been so angry in her life. He had hurt an innocent man, ruined years of her work, and threatened all of their lives here in a dangerous past, and he had joked about it.

Joked.

Like it was all one big lark.

She was breathing hard. Then she moved toward him again, but Jeff grabbed her.

"No," he said.

"I'm not going to kill him," she said.

Instead, she dumped out the bundle, then ripped the linen in half.

Thomas had raised one hand to his forehead, and he was moaning. Either she had injured him badly or he figured she wasn't going to attack him any longer.

She handed the ripped cloth to Jeff. Then she grabbed Thomas's hands and pulled them together.

"Tie him as tightly as you can," she said.

Jeff blinked at her.

"Do it!" she snapped. She wasn't sure how long she could hold Thomas.

Jeff tied the linen around Thomas's wrists so tightly that she could see the fabric digging into his skin.

"Now what do we do with him?" Jeff asked.

"Give me a minute," she said, "and I'll figure it out."

———

For a moment, Thomas thought he was vindicated. Even though his head hurt so badly he could barely move and the pain in his spine traveled all the way through his legs, he figured he would survive this.

When the guards or whoever found him and untied him, he would twist away, grab his little remote and vanish.

He would be gambling that this room would still be in Martin Tower in the future, but it was a small gamble. They usually didn't change the configuration of an existing Tower.

Besides, anything would be better than staying here.

Neyla picked up the Jewels and put them back. Then she stood up, putting one hand on her own spine.

In the other hand, she held his knife.

———

Thomas's eyes widened. He clearly thought she was going to kill him.

She wasn't going to kill him. She wasn't that kind of woman. She wasn't even going to damage his handsome mocking face, although she was still tempted.

He had no idea how much work he was going to cause her.

Somehow she had to drag him out of here. And then they were going to have to deal with him in the future.

She had no idea what would come of that.

But first, she had to make everything right.

She handed the knife to Jeff. Then she untied her own bundle, added Thomas's things to it as she looked for the unauthorized tools he had brought along. Something had gotten him into this building, and he had used something to hurt that guard.

She didn't see anything that would fit those descriptions in his bundle.

Which meant they were on him.

Smart. He might have had to leave the bundle behind. He clearly planned ahead.

She opened his jacket then ripped open his shirt.

The disk rested against his chest. But that wasn't what caught her attention.

What caught her attention was everything he had smuggled in. Skeleton key, extra knife, stun gun, and a dark, dingy ring.

She grabbed the ring.

It was heavy, ugly, and old. She rubbed her finger across it, removing layers of dirt. A gigantic sapphire gleamed up at her.

Edward the Confessor's ring.

But she had seen it in the cupboard.

Gleaming prettily.

Because it came from the 21st century, polished, and shiny. Not because it belonged here.

Because it was paste.

"You son of a bitch," she said. She turned to the cupboard, grabbed the fake ring, and put the original back.

Then she bent over and grabbed the remote, holding it in her hand.

Thomas looked frightened for the first time. "Don't," he said.

"You think I'm going to leave you here?" she asked.

"You can't," Jeff said. "He doesn't fit."

"Don't take that," Thomas said. He wasn't quite begging. She wasn't sure if she wanted him to beg. She didn't want to see him lose all of his dignity.

"Give me one good reason why I shouldn't," she said.

His eyes moved back and forth, as he clearly thought of several options and discarded them. Finally, he said, "You'd be sentencing me to death. You're not that kind of woman."

"Sentencing you to death," she mused. "Here, in the Tower of London."

His cheeks flushed a dark red. She could feel the fear coming off him in waves. He actually believed she might leave him here.

Instead, she let the remote fall back onto his chest.

"Come here, Jeff," she said. "We're going to have to carry him out."

"I can walk," Thomas said.

"So get up," she said.

He rocked, moaned, and was about to work his way up when Jeff grabbed an arm, yanking him to his feet.

"We're not going to let you go anywhere unescorted," Jeff said.

Neyla took the paste ring and all of the tools, putting them in her bundle. Then she left the remains of Thomas's bundle. There was no way to hide the fact that he had broken into the cupboard.

But nothing was missing. So if the guard was smart, he could take credit for chasing the robber away.

Lots of ifs.

She took Thomas's other arm. Then she and Jeff dragged him out of the cupboard room, and back to the stairs.

Thomas thought of fighting, but he was outnumbered, and she had hurt him.

He wasn't sure he blamed her. He had destroyed her life's work.

Damn. He should have escaped. If she had only taken a few minutes longer to reach the cupboard, he probably would have escaped.

If she had been a different kind of woman, he would have asked her to join him. Who could tell if the Confessor's ring was different? He would have wagered no one had tested that sapphire in hundreds of years. Besides, modern paste sapphires weren't made of plastic. They were crystals too, just not quite as valuable as the real thing.

But he knew better than to argue. Besides, what could they do to him? When they got back to the 21st century, it would be their word against his. And even if they convinced the folks at Portals that he had tried to steal the Jewels, it didn't matter. The crime occurred hundreds of years in the past.

No one could prosecute him.

No one would dare.

Or so he told himself as he let them drag him up the stairs, back to the door, and—he hoped—the future.

———————

Neyla's heart was pounding. Adrenaline still poured through her system. She wanted to move fast, but didn't dare.

The others were waiting at the top of the staircase. Benedict looked terrified. Dan just seemed nervous. He kept turning his head, as if expecting someone to attack them at any moment.

But if no one had come when the guard was attacked, then no one was going to come at all. One thing about thick stone walls. They were mostly soundproof.

Dan took Thomas from her. Neither he nor Benedict seemed surprised that they had captured Thomas or that he looked a little roughed up.

They led him through the corridor as if this had been the plan all along. The guard was still prone. But he had raised one hand to his head and he was moaning.

They had to hurry.

Neyla pushed open the doors. The air outside was cooler but smellier.

It was still dark. Somehow she had expected the sun to be coming up. It seemed like she had been in Martin Tower for hours, and it had probably been less than thirty minutes.

She made Jeff extinguish his candle, then the five of them hurried across the grounds. She kept an eye out for the guard who had made his rounds earlier, but she didn't see him.

When she reached the spot where the team had arrived, she almost told them to get their remotes.

Then she realized that they were feet lower than they had been. They might materialize inside the ground.

For a moment, she felt at a complete loss. The plan had been to find a safe place, figure out the guard schedule, and get out at the right time.

She didn't have time. She had no idea what the right place was now.

The others stared at her.

Then she realized what she had to do.

She opened the bundle and pulled out the skeleton key she had taken from Thomas.

"We're going inside," she said.

They didn't disagree. Because they knew they had no choice.

———

It only took a few minutes to find a door, and get them inside. She was heading to the one place she knew hadn't changed in all the centuries of the White Tower's existence: the Chapel of St. John.

It was up several floors, but she had no trouble getting there. The team ran into no guards, no locked doors. The White Tower's interior looked pretty much the same now as it would centuries in the future.

The others followed her without question, dragging

Thomas with them. For once, he had nothing to say. No quips, no barbs, no suggestions. He just let them take him back to the future.

She wasn't sure she liked this subdued Thomas any more than she liked the arrogant man she had first met. But she wasn't going to worry about him at the moment.

She led the group up stairs and through dingy corridors to the Chapel of St. John. Under the impressive Norman arches, candles burned on the altar. Votive candles, in memory of someone. The Church of England had picked up a lot of habits from the Catholic Church and continued to practice them, for which she was very grateful.

Because the altar itself looked unchanged to her.

She looked at her group. They were filthy from running through dirty corridors. Thomas's jaw had marks from her fingertips. Jeff actually had some blood on his face, but whether that was from her or from Thomas, she didn't know.

"Ready to go home?" she asked.

They nodded.

She would have to untie Thomas so that he could use his remote.

She leaned toward him. "Try anything, and one of us will take that remote and leave you here."

He looked up at her. "Have a little compassion," he said. "You're in a church."

She grabbed his remote. "I mean it," she said.

He sighed. "I'll be a good boy."

She nodded. Then she untied his hands.

They all grabbed their remotes. As she nodded, they pressed the activation switches.

And everything went dark.

The wind came up, but it didn't blow hot and cold this time. It blew softly, marking her movement. The smell barely changed either, but maybe she couldn't smell anything after having been in that stinky place.

Then she stopped moving and stumbled against the altar. Jeff stumbled against her. Dan staggered forward, and Benedict fell onto a chair.

Thomas landed in a heap on the floor beside her. His face had turned white. He really was in terrible shape.

No candles burned. Pews extended in front of her and beyond them, one of the Yeoman Warders peered inside.

Her heart jumped.

Had they been caught? Were they going to be arrested?

Then she realized it didn't matter.

The worst thing they had done would be to have stayed past closing time. If the remotes had worked properly, they would have arrived here only a second or two later than they left.

In an entirely different part of the Tower.

"We're closing up," the Yeoman Warder said in very understandable modern British English. "That includes the gift shop. If you want to buy something for home, I'd suggest leaving now. You've got a bit of a walk ahead of you."

"Thank you," Neyla said. Her voice sounded wheezy. She was still lightheaded.

The Warder went back into the corridor, his message delivered.

Jeff grabbed Thomas's arms. Neyla retied his wrists, then leaned against him. "Try anything, and I'll have you arrested."

"For what?" he asked.

"Whatever I can think of," she said, not conceding that he had a good point. What could they do to him? His crime was in the past. Unless he had completed a major identity theft.

Thomas Ayliffe couldn't be his real name.

They secured him. Then they grouped around him—Jeff and Benedict on each side, Dan behind, using his body to hide Thomas's tied hands. Neyla stayed a few yards ahead, just in case something came at them.

They didn't say anything as they trooped down the aisle, out of the chapel, and into the Inner Ward, heading back to the gate.

Heading home.

————

He had a concussion, a bruised tailbone, and cracked ribs. Thomas lay on cool hospital sheets where he was being kept for observation. He had a private room, courtesy of Portals, and a security guard, also courtesy of Portals.

He wasn't to talk to anyone outside of the company.

He wasn't sure if that was ever or just for the duration.

All he did know was that the hospital wanted him here for observation since, they believed, he'd had quite a fall when he was urban free climbing with Dan.

As if Thomas would ever do anything that stupid.

He wasn't supposed to close his eyes, but he was tired. Tired and disappointed. So close. He'd actually held the Jewels in his hand. How many modern thieves could say that they had touched the Crown Jewels?

Although touching wasn't nearly enough.

And he wasn't going to be able to go back to his sponsor and make another attempt.

He had failed. His first big failure.

And he doubted Portals would ever let anyone get that close again.

At least he wasn't going to jail. Wycroft had told him that much during his short visit here. Thomas wasn't going to jail because they couldn't prove identity theft and everything else would be "too incredible for any local magistrate to adjudicate."

Thank heavens.

So Thomas, once he healed, would be escorted out of the hospital, out of London, and away from any Portals site forever.

Although he had seen enough of their systems to know that forever might not be that long. Since his sponsor still had people inside, and Thomas did know the system.

He wouldn't get near the Crown Jewels again. At least, not in 1674. And he wasn't going near Neyla.

But if he remembered right, Henry VIII had sold some of the Jewels to pay for his various wars. Maybe, if Thomas figured out the right way to approach things, he could try again.

Years from now.

If he wanted to put in the work.

Which he really wasn't sure he did.

———

Neyla stood in her window, looking down on the Tower Bridge, and the Tower itself.

She would be going back, after she had a ton of allergy shots, once she figured out when would be a good time. She couldn't go anywhere near the first of July, thanks to Thomas. That assault on the guard hadn't made it into the history books and, so far as she could tell, had no impact on history itself. But it would harm her little band if they returned at the wrong moment.

Now, at least, she could wait until Pete was well. She'd have her original team back.

Thank heavens. She wouldn't have to worry about another Thomas Ayliffe.

She had tried to visit him in the hospital, but Wycroft had cordoned him off. Ayliffe was leaving London as soon as he was able, which angered her.

He would be a free man.

Because they couldn't prove identity theft. His identification was rock-solid, no matter how much she believed he had made up the name. They couldn't charge him with corporate espionage, not without divulging a few too many corporate secrets, and they couldn't charge him with any other crime.

In fact, Wycroft pointed out to Neyla, she was the one who faced legal charges. She had assaulted Ayliffe in front of a witness.

In 1674. Because he had made her completely and utterly furious.

She had expected to learn things while in the past. She just hadn't expected to learn she was capable of such violence.

It disturbed her less than it probably should have. She should have been appalled. But she had always known that humans had a base nature. She figured people in the past were closer to it than people of her generation.

But she had proven her own assumptions wrong.

Without that base nature, the Tower wouldn't exist. And she wouldn't have the bones of Princes to investigate.

Maybe she should thank Ayliffe. He had taught her that the past could be dangerous and unexpected—and so could she.

NEWSLETTER SIGN-UP

DEAN WESLEY SMITH

Sign up for the Dean Wesley Smith newsletter, and keep up with the latest news, releases and so much more—even the occasional giveaway.

Go to **deanwesleysmith.com.**

Sign up for the WMG Publishing newsletter, too, and get the latest news and releases from all of the WMG authors and lines, including *Pulphouse Fiction Magazine, Smith's Monthly,* and so much more.

To sign up go to **wmgpublishing.com**.

Follow Dean on BookBub

ABOUT THE EDITOR

DEAN WESLEY SMITH

Considered one of the most prolific writers working in modern fiction, with more than 30 million books sold, *USA Today* bestselling writer Dean Wesley Smith published far more than a hundred novels in forty years, and hundreds of short stories across many genres.

At the moment he produces novels in several major series, including the time travel Thunder Mountain novels set in the Old West, the galaxy-spanning Seeders Universe series, the urban fantasy Ghost of a Chance series, a superhero series starring Poker Boy, and a mystery series featuring the retired detectives of the Cold Poker Gang.

His monthly magazine, *Smith's Monthly*, which consists of only his own fiction, premiered in October 2013 and offers readers more than 70,000 words per issue, including a new and original novel every month.

During his career, Dean also wrote a couple dozen *Star Trek* novels, the only two original *Men in Black* novels, Spider-Man and X-Men novels, plus novels set in gaming and television worlds. Writing with his wife Kristine Kathryn Rusch under the name Kathryn Wesley, he wrote the novel for the NBC miniseries The Tenth Kingdom and other books for *Hallmark Hall of Fame* movies.

He wrote novels under dozens of pen names in the worlds of comic books and movies, including novelizations of almost a dozen films, from *The Final Fantasy* to *Steel* to *Rundown*.

Dean also worked as a fiction editor off and on, starting at Pulphouse Publishing, then at *VB Tech Journal*, then Pocket Books, and now at WMG Publishing, where he and Kristine Kathryn Rusch serve as series editors for the acclaimed *Fiction River* anthology series.

For more information about Dean's books and ongoing projects, please visit his website at www.deanwesley-smith.com and sign up for his newsletter.

For more information:
www.deanwesleysmith.com

facebook.com/deanwsmith3
patreon.com/deanwesleysmith
bookbub.com/authors/dean-wesley-smith

www.ingramcontent.com/pod-product-compliance
Lightning Source LLC
Chambersburg PA
CBHW010729100726
47899CB00009B/2989